GOLD FOR THE DEAD

ANN APTAKER

Bywater
BOOKS

2025

Bywater Books

Copyright © 2025 Ann Aptaker

Print ISBN: 978-1-61294-327-5

Bywater Books First Edition: October 2025

Printed in the United States of America on acid-free paper.

Cover designer: TreeHouse Studio

Bywater Books
PO Box 3671
Ann Arbor MI 48106-3671
www.bywaterbooks.com

This novel is a work of fiction.

*This book is dedicated to everyone who has
gone the distance for a friend.*

Chapter One

Early November, 1958
New York City
6 p.m.

Trust is a hard thing to come by. Most people, even the nicest people, the type of people who give potluck dinners and watch each other's kids, they'll give you the shaft if it means they come out on top, or if they just don't have time for you. Can't blame them, really. Life's a tough game. A handful of people win. Most just get by. Everybody else loses. Too many people, even those nice people, want to put me into the losing slot because of the way I dress—a dame in gentlemen's suits—and my preference for the love and lust of women.

It's the same story in my outlaw world, just a lot more dangerous. Greed backed up by guns does a lot of the talking. To stay alive I have to stay sharp, because every time I steal a painting, a fancy jewel, or some other treasure and smuggle it into town for clients who are generally the winners of life's crap game, I have to navigate a treacherous maze of dirty dealing. So when I find anyone who's the real deal, who not only keeps their word but knows what the word is, I value their life as much as my own.

Nick Fortunato is the real deal, a guy with a big heart and a sincere soul. I've known him all my life, since we were kids in Coney Island. Nick spent our childhood years hanging around back alley dice games hidden behind the thrill rides, fortune-teller rackets, and Coney's shooting galleries. He kept his eye on the action, his young head for numbers picking up on the odds and how to beat them.

I spent those same tender years pillaging trinkets from beach bags and storing the loot under the boardwalk until I had enough to haul a sack onto the subway to Manhattan, where I'd fence the stuff. These days, I pillage more expensive trinkets from fancier and faraway places, sometimes from museums, galleries, and rich art collectors, just as often for them. Nick's come a long way, too. He's become a big-time, big-money bookie, known in the trade as Nicky Fast Hands for the fast payouts he makes when your horse comes in or your team wins, and the fast grabs he makes for your dollar when your horse craps out or your team falls on its face. His players trust him, though. They know he gives honest counts, no funny business.

For the last several years on Nick's birthday, from the time we both started making real dough, I bring a couple of bottles of good Italian wine to his apartment and give him a sawbuck to place a bet on a nag we both know won't win. And every year on my birthday, he brings me a couple of bottles of Chivas Regal scotch and places a ten-dollar bet for me on a horse he knows will pay off.

Today is Nick's birthday. I'll pull a tenner from my wallet for the bet on a losing nag in tonight's trotters at Yonkers Raceway. Nick will phone it in from his apartment to his bookie parlor in the basement of a Front Street warehouse, near the downtown East River docks. Then we'll order in a big Italian meal from a neighborhood red sauce joint, drink both bottles of the pricey

Barolo I've brought for his birthday, and gossip about who's scored big and who got pinched in our shared underworld. Sooner or later we'll lapse into memories of the old days when we were trouble-making kids back in Coney Island. Somewhere around midnight, both of us a little rubbery after the heavy meal and finishing off both bottles of wine, I'll get sentimental about the time he saved my teenage life, yanked me so hard out of the path of an oncoming truck I slammed into half-a-dozen pedestrians behind me, sending a couple of guys to the pavement. Nick shielded me when one of those guys, a big lug, came at me with fists and nasty remarks about my clothes; a rather snappy yellow shirt and blue tie paired with my dungarees. Nick got me out of there fast when the cops arrived to break things up.

I won't be the only sentimental slob tonight, though. The wine, as always, will bring out the loyal softie in Nick. Around the same time I'm wallowing in memories of him saving me from a beating probably followed by an arrest, Nick will raise his empty wine glass in a toast and say, "To us and all our drunken birthdays," and that it's always been okay by him that "you dress the way you do, and damn if you don't look swell in those silk suits. Even those scars on your face give you a certain rough class. Hell, you earned 'em, Cantor." He says it every year. I like hearing it every year.

I park my Buick, the latest black-and-cream two-toner stretched out in the new sleek style—though I do miss the curvier models of just a few years ago—and look forward the annual birthday ritual with Nick. For the occasion, I'm decked out in a royal blue suit, white shirt, finished off with a deep-green-and-yellow checked tie and a deep green pocket square. I did the best I could with my always unruly short brown hair, which I've begun to notice is sprouting threads of gray here and there. The birthdays are catching up to me.

The November night is clear, the wind cold and brisk. I turn up the collar of my overcoat and pull the brim of my tweed cap down low while I walk the half block from my car to Nick's apartment. He lives on West Eleventh Street, a neighborhood of ritzy eighteenth- and nineteenth-century Neo-Classical and Federal style townhouses just off lower Fifth Avenue. The light of streetlamps picks out the details of front stoops with ornate ironwork, marble lintels over windows, and entry doors of carved wood with brass handles. Branches of the now leafless sycamore trees along the curb are etched into the night sky like bony fingers grabbing for the moon.

Nick's building, built sometime in the 1920s, is one of only two apartment houses on the block. The building isn't a sore-thumb job, though. The brick face running up all nine floors is just as dignified as the brick of the Old Money residences beside it. The columned white marble of its Neo-Classical entrance calms the neighbors' fears that the building's tenants might be two-bit upstarts moving in on the local aristocracy. People like Nick Fortunato.

The lobby's pretty silk-stocking, too; black and white tile floor, pale peach walls with sconces of frosted glass flower petals that give the place a creamy glow. The mahogany-paneled elevator adds another touch of class, the kind of class Nick and I dreamed of as kids and can finally afford. Money and its privileges is the revenge we take on the snoots who still don't like us: Nick for his immigrant parentage, me for mine, and for my strutting around town in custom-tailored suits, often with the pleasure of a woman on my arm.

I wonder—and laugh to myself—as I ride up the elevator, what'll be the name of the horse I'll lose money on tonight. I can already picture Nick's chummy but mischievous grin when he palms my sawbuck. Happy birthday, Nicky-o.

The elevator arrives at the ninth floor and I step out into the hallway, its rosy glow an echo of the lobby décor. Thick black carpeting silences my footsteps.

At Nick's apartment, I press the door buzzer, ready to greet the birthday boy. I've got a bottle of wine under each arm.

A minute passes and he doesn't answer.

I buzz again, back it up with a knock on the door, but when nothing comes of it I try the doorknob.

The door's not locked, which gives me an uneasy feeling. Leaving apartment doors unlocked is not your typical New York habit. I open it, walk inside, accompanied by a horde of butterflies flying around in my stomach.

The vestibule light is on, and so are the table lamps in the living room, a beige linen wallpaper-lined room decked out in the latest modern furnishings. Wine glasses are set out on the kidney-shaped glass-topped coffee table. Today's racing form lies haphazardly on the couch, a sleek item upholstered in discreet red-and-light-gray horizontal stripes. A small, cozy fire is going in a fireplace set into a white brick wall.

I call out, "Nick?" hoping he'll walk in from the kitchen with a smile on his face and maybe a cannoli in his hand.

Silence. The kind of silence that sends those butterflies into a frenzy.

I set the wine bottles down on the coffee table, and that's when I see the dark reddish stain smeared on the charcoal gray carpet below one of the table legs. The leg's polished steel reflects the stain, making it look even more gruesome.

In my dangerous line of work with dangerous people, I know the difference between wine stains and bloodstains. This one ain't a wine stain. When I reach down to touch it, it's warm, damp, and sticky.

My jaw tightens and my throat swallows hard, reactions against the horror movie the bloodstain triggers in my mind.

I pull myself out of the horror movie and get to work trying to find a more sane explanation for the blood on the carpet. Maybe Nick broke a wine glass and cut himself. Maybe he caught his hand or his knee on something, and maybe I'm grasping at nonexistent straws. The blood on the carpet didn't come from a scratch or cut or any other clumsy wound. The smeared blood on the carpet came from something much more brutal.

I work fast. It takes me less than ten minutes to give the apartment the once-over, check for signs of struggle or any trace of what happened here, who made it happen, and what happened to Nick. I start in the kitchen, look for any blood smears on the white cabinets and green-and-white checkered linoleum floor, thinking that maybe Nick took the fight in here, but the kitchen's clean.

So is the bathroom. There's no trace of blood on the aqua wall tiles, no smudges in the sink or tub or shower stall, the flamingos etched into its glass door clean and dry. There's nothing to indicate that Nick or someone else washed blood off the walls or their hands.

In the bedroom, Nick's bed is unruffled, the stripes of its blue and yellow bedspread straight as the columns in Nick's ledger books of payouts and pay-ups. Nothing's been knocked over on the cherrywood night tables. The bedside lamps, with the new style of rocket-shaped white glass globes, are still upright. The electric alarm clock is on its base and humming away. The mirror over the sleek bureau is unbroken, and the stuff on the bureau— an orange glass vase shaped like a tall, skinny raindrop, an empty blue glass ashtray heavy enough to brain someone, and a green ceramic dish with a pair of pearl cufflinks and a pair of gold ones—are all undisturbed.

All I'm sure of after I look over everything in the apartment and wipe my fingerprints from anything I've touched before I leave, taking the two wine bottles with me, is that the bloodstain on the living room carpet is a sure bet that Nick didn't walk out of here on his own. He might not have walked at all.

The bright lights and high energy of my Theater District

neighborhood welcome me home, even giving me the gift of a parking spot down the block from my place. But even my neighborhood's neon lights and snappy crowds headed to the jazz joints and Broadway shows can't lift my worry about what might've happened to a guy I've shared a lifetime with, a childhood of scraped knees on hard streets and last laughs won when we survived dicey adventures.

Pretty soon, when the winners of today's racing and sports action don't get paid off and the losers are strangely left alone, word will get around that Fast Hands Nick Fortunato is missing. Some underworld rats will crawl out of their holes to make a play for any money Nick was supposed to pay out. Other rats will scurry back into their holes to avoid paying up their losses to whoever takes over Nick's book.

None of those rats scare me. They're just money sniffers, running toward the scent of free-floating cash, or running from the ravenous rats out to grab it. Only two types of rats give me the willies: one is the guy who bankrolled Nick when he opened his shop and who's taken a cut of his action ever since, and the other is the deadliest gang of rats in town, the cops. The first rat doesn't care how I live, as long as I come up with the goods when he wants me to. The second set of rats, the cops, have been doing their best for years to put me away on any charge they can, especially a morals charge. They'd really like to hang me with that one. The boys in blue would sneer on my way to the slammer.

Upstairs in my apartment, I pour myself a stiff scotch to settle my mind and my nerves. I leave the living room lamps off and cozy up with the whiskey in my favorite big red club chair. Neon light from the marquees of the jazz joints and the nearby Broadway theaters drifts through my windows. The colors float around my living room and across my glass of scotch, turning the whiskey into a fantasy potion.

The good whiskey, the dreamy light, and the warm familiarity of home don't do a damn thing to calm my fears for Nick, a guy who's been true blue with me when a helluva lot of people, especially those very nice people, have wanted me to shut up, disappear, or drop dead. Nick never judged about how I live my life, about who I wine, dine, and bed. He never turned his back on me, even when it might've been smart to do so. Nick stayed that real deal, and now he's missing, maybe dead. Or maybe not, I hope. Maybe just bloodied.

Each sip of the scotch opens up more of me, unlocks memories of me and Nick and our childhood mischief and our rogue adulthood. Each swallow of the whiskey finds the truth in my soul that I can't just sit around and stew. I have to find out what happened to Nick. Otherwise, the few loyalties and friends one makes in my tough world—hell, the few true friends anyone makes at all—would mean nothing. That's too cold a life, even for a tough dyke like me.

I pour myself another scotch, let my mind cycle through various possibilities of where to start, who to talk to, which rat holes to crawl through, but I'm jolted back into the here and now by the ringing phone. I figure maybe if I ignore it, sooner or later the caller will give up. I'm in no mood for social calls or calls from potential clients or any kind of chitchat at all.

The damn phone keeps ringing until it annoys me enough that I finally get up from the chair and answer it. My simple, "Yeah?" is countered with a man's gravelly voice and slow way of talking that makes my ears prickle and my throat tighten.

Every word, few as they are, is soaked with threat. It's the voice of one of the rats who scare the hell out of me. "Stay out of it, Cantor," he says.

Chapter Two

When Sig Loreale, the town's most powerful and ruthless crime boss, tells you to stay out of it, the smart types, the types who value their lives, stay out of it. But after a rotten evening and two strong whiskies, I'm feeling more surly than smart. "Stay out of what, Sig?"

"You know very well what I am talking about," he says. Sig has this habit of speaking so slowly that you're shaking either with frustration or fear by the time he reaches the end of his sentence. I've known Sig a long time, ever since he muscled his way into the old Coney Island rackets when Nick and I were kids. I know him long enough to know when he's being intentionally threatening and when he's just being his scary, ice cold self.

Right now, I peg it the latter. "You're gonna have to spell it out for me, Sig."

"Stop it, Cantor. It is not like you to be stupid. You know very well that I am talking about your friend Mr. Fortunato. You were at his apartment tonight for his birthday. You always go to his apartment on his birthday. And he goes to your apartment on yours."

Yeah, there it is, the big shot Sig Loreale, the guy with so much power, so much influence, so many threads spread so far and woven so deep that he knows what goes on everywhere in this city and beyond. He even knows who's doing it, and when they're doing it.

Still, I venture out on a dangerously swaying branch, because at the end of that branch might be a scrap of information about what happened to Nick. "Oh, you mean my friend the bookie who's missing? Whose apartment has blood on the living room rug? Did you have him killed, Sig?"

It takes an exasperatingly long time for Sig to finish saying, "Mr. Fortunato is not dead." The only thing missing from that sentence is the word "yet."

"I'm glad to hear it," I say, more relieved than I dare let him know. "So why did your boys grab him? As far as I know, he's been sending you your cut of the action every week like clockwork. Only a fool would hold out on you, Sig, and Nick Fortunato is no fool. So what's your beef with him?"

"Perhaps you have not been listening to me, Cantor. I have instructed you to stay out of this situation regarding Mr. Fortunato. It is for your own good."

There's a click and then the line goes dead. I hear nothing except hissing silence, and the warning that comes with it.

The best way for me to get the better of that hissing silence and not let Sig scare me more than usual is to pull a .38 revolver from the wall safe in my bedroom, fill the gun's chambers, slip the gun's shoulder rig under my suit jacket, and put a handful of extra ammo into my trouser pocket. Back out in the hall, I take my overcoat and tweed cap from the closet and walk out of my apartment, the .38 snug and warm in its rig under my arm.

It's time to teach Sig Loreale a lesson in friendship.

It's almost eight o'clock by the time I park my Buick by the East River's downtown docks. The wind coming off the river is cold as steel teeth, its bite a reminder to the neighborhood locals of just how much their lives are at the mercy of the river, how much their survival depends on the maritime trade and the racketeers who have it in their grip. It's the perfect neighborhood for a bookie joint. Down here, where the long-ago enterprise of building the Brooklyn Bridge once promised progress and the good life in a modern future, the Gothic arches of its stone towers now rise into the sky with a majesty at odds with the backbreaking lives of the longshoremen, the crooked labor bosses who own them, and the rough pleasures to be found in the waterfront saloons. Hovering over everything is the slow clang of the river's buoy bells and the deep bellow of ships' horns, a mournful soundtrack to the grinding and dangerous lives lived around here.

Front Street is a shadowy, cobblestoned thoroughfare of old brick warehouses muscled between equally old four- and five-story brick tenements whose rusting fire escapes serve as laundry racks, a place to air rugs, and outdoor sleeping quarters in the city's sweltering slum summers. You won't find air conditioners sticking out of the tenement windows come July. Nobody around here has the kind of dough to afford them.

Half of the curbside streetlamps are dark, busted out by certain citizens who don't want other citizens to see what they're doing. It's to everyone's benefit that no one on Front Street even bothers to notice the traffic of humanity of every race and class—some in well-tailored suits and coats, some in workman's clothes, some even in shabby, nearly dead duds—that day and night walks down the old cast iron stairs to the basement of a hulking warehouse at the corner of Front and Dover Streets. No one even gives me a sideways glance as I pass under one of the few working streetlamps, my shadow sliding around me, or when I walk down the steps to the warehouse's basement door.

After a couple of knocks, a dark-skinned, gray-haired black man, a guy I know, opens the door. His name's Freddie Holmes. He used to run his own bookie joint up in Harlem until another operator, a white guy with bigger guns, a bigger gang, and even bigger connections, moved in on Freddie, literally tossing him into the street. Nick, never one to pass up good talent, recruited Freddie for the door job down here because no one can judge who's kosher and who's not better than Freddie Holmes.

He runs his thumbs under his suspenders, his white shirt picking up glare from the single overhead lightbulb. The grin he gives me is more or less friendly, the flesh of his face wrinkling like an old leather bag, a bag that holds years of smarts and secrets. "Cantor Gold," he says by way of bare bones greeting. "Bad night to come down here, or haven't you heard?"

"Yeah, I heard," I say, and leave it at that. I like Freddie, and I'm pretty sure I can trust him, but the fewer people who know I was at Nick's apartment with only a bloodstain for company, or that Sig Loreale is involved, the better. "Look, Freddie, that's why I'm here, to see if anyone knows anything that might help me find out what happened to Nick."

He gives me one of his famous look-'em-over hard stares, his eyes slitted now with cagey curiosity. "Why you stickin' your nose in it, Cantor?"

"Nick's a friend," I say, "a good a friend who's stood by me since we were kids. I could always count on Nick and he could always count on me. Maybe he's counting on me now. Isn't that enough?"

It takes Freddie a second or two of serious thought. Then he drops the hard stare and nods his head as he snaps his suspenders against his shirt. "Sure, sure," he says with emotion under it. "Loyalties gotta mean somethin' or livin' is just too hard. Well, c'mon in, Cantor. But I gotta tell you, there's no action, no bets. Everyone's been taken off the phones and the wires. The boys are takin' the whole place apart."

"So soon? Isn't that a little cold?"

"What's the matter with you, Cantor? You been around. Don't you know what's goin' on? Word's already spread that Nick's gone missin'. That means the cops are gonna know about it pretty quick, and figure that they won't get their cut of the take this week, maybe not for a lotta weeks, maybe forever. Next thing you know, the cops will be down here flashin' their badges, askin' a lotta questions, shakin' everyone down, nosin' around for information, just like you're doin'." He finishes that with a smile I can't quite read. I'm not meant to.

"Yeah, but nobody wants to spill to a cop," I say.

"You think you stand a better chance?"

With a *tsk* that implies a maybe, and a shrug that admits I don't know, I walk past Freddie and through a door with blacked-out glass.

Beyond the door is a large, dimly lit room busy with guys in shirtsleeves, some guys wearing fedoras or flat caps, some wearing green eyeshades. Everybody is either packing up the rows of telephones on long tables, disconnecting teletype machines, or ripping up race result lists and betting slips and burning them in trash baskets. A couple of guys, including Mike Landers, the leader of the crew that handles the phoned-in bets, are stacking chairs in a small gallery area where bettors who like to win and lose their money in person lounge around with racing forms and sports sheets. Mike's a wiry guy, slender as a log and just as solid.

Three other guys, led by chubby-faced odds-master Chickie D'Andrea, are up and down ladders in front of a wall of blackboards, erasing the odds numbers from racetracks and sports arenas all over the country.

A few guys give me a wave or a nod, but most just keep working to pack up Nick's bookie joint before the cops show up asking questions nobody is in the mood to answer.

I'm not interested in questioning any of these guys, at least not yet. Instead, I make my way to the office at the side of the room.

A picture window takes up most of the office wall, the better to keep an eye on the action in the main room. Inside, a woman who really knows how to wear a light blue pullover sweater, slender brown skirt, and a wide leather black belt that moves around her body as if carving fine sculpture, is busy emptying her desk and boxing up ledger books. Her name's Abby O'Neill, and there have probably been as many side bets on who she runs around with after hours as there have been bets on the horses or football games. But nobody's ever won the bet because Abby never tells.

The only things I know about Abby are that she shares Nick's trait of a head for numbers, that she's as efficient as a time clock, that her father used to be muscle for the West Side Irish mob until he met his end at the point a knife on the docks, and that Nick trusts her completely to run the day-to-day operations of his bookie business. My eyes tell me the rest: her eyes, catlike in shape, are dark and liquid as an exotic sea; her full lips inspire fantasies that make parts of me tingle; and her short, wavy dark brunette almost black hair softly frames a face that hints at danger as well as a zest for life.

I take my cap off, run my fingers through my always unruly short brown hair, and knock on the glass-paned door just for the pleasure of having Abby look up from her labors and hear her wine-smooth drawl, "Come in, Cantor." Once I'm inside, she says, "Steal any nice paintings lately?"

"Why? Are you in the market? I'd empty the Louvre for you, Abby, you know that." I give her my best courtly grin.

"I'll keep it in mind," she says, enjoying the banter before coming around to the front of her desk and getting us back to business. "I suppose Freddie filled you in?"

I give that a nod, take out my pack of Chesterfields and lighter from my inside suit jacket pocket, and shake out a cigarette for Abby. She pulls it from the pack, her red nail polish catching a glint from the overhead light fixture. I light her smoke, then light one for myself.

She takes a deep drag, exhales, her eyes piercing the smoke

as she leans against the desk. She looks me over the way a cat stares at a new toy and decides if it suits its mood. "I bet you didn't tell Freddie you were at Nick's place," she says. Reading my quizzical look, Abby adds with a canny smile that could pull every thought from my brain, "It's Nick's birthday. You two always get together on your birthdays."

"He told you that?"

"Sure, he told me that. He also said that he looked forward to those drunken evenings. So why are you here, Cantor?"

There's a folding chair opposite her desk. I sit down in it and look up at Abby. It's like looking up at a masterpiece of Classical sculpture. "Listen, Abby, Nick was already gone by the time I showed up at his apartment. The door was unlocked. That was the first sign of trouble, so I let myself in. Nothing was out of place, there were no signs of struggle except for blood on the living room carpet. I don't know what happened to Nick or where he is, but I know who does, and you won't like it."

She looks straight down at me, her eyes bright, her body stiff, her expression telling me she's figured something she wishes she hadn't but can't get rid of. When she finally says the name, "Sig?" her voice is a near whisper.

I give her a slow nod. "Have you heard from him?"

"No, not yet." She takes another drag on her cigarette, a long drag followed by a long exhale. But even the cloud of exhaled smoke can't hide the tension in her face. Whatever's going on behind her eyes are pictures and thoughts she won't let me see. "Who else could it be?" she finally says. "Sig Loreale is Nick's. . . well, I guess you could say he's Nick's silent partner. I have to calculate Sig's cut every week and take the envelope to him myself."

"And the cops' cut?"

"Sure, I figure that, too, and give Sig the tally. But what makes you think he knows what happened to Nick, or where he is?"

I don't answer right away, but use a long pull on my own

smoke as an excuse for my silence. I need a moment to think, to figure how much to share with Abby before she forks over any information she might have that I don't about Nick and Sig's business relationship.

It's not long, though, before I arrive at the only destination there is on this road: I have to give in order to get. And besides, since Nick trusts Abby, I guess I have to, too. "Because Sig phoned me," I say. "He warned me to stay out of it, and when I dangled the idea that his boys might've killed Nick, he assured me that Nick is still alive."

"So Loreale has him?" Her sigh is shallow, edgy. I can't blame her for being scared. Abby is smart enough to be scared of Sig.

"I don't know if Sig has him," I say. "And it seems Sig has his reasons to keep Nick alive. Maybe if we knew those reasons we can figure why Nick's been grabbed, either by Sig or by someone else. And then maybe we can figure how to get Nick back. Look, Abby, you know a lot about the business between Nick and Sig. Any idea why Sig or anyone else would want to grab him?"

She crushes out her cigarette in the ashtray on the desk with a nervous hand. "No. I have no idea."

"Are you sure?"

"Of course I'm sure."

I'm fast out of the chair, stand close to Abby, close enough feel her breath, see the spark of anger in her eyes. "Abby, you crushed out that cigarette like you were afraid your hand would catch fire. Something about Nick's disappearance and Sig's involvement scares you. What is it?"

She escapes me by walking around to the other side of her desk and busies herself with piles of papers again, putting them in a box, and stacking a group of ledgers. Her red nail polish shines like blood spots against the black ledger books. "Look, Cantor," she says but doesn't look at me, "I don't know what Sig has in mind about Nick, and it's probably better if I don't know. Same goes for you. I don't know why you're poking around in

Sig's business, anyway. If and when Sig wants me to know, he'll tell me. If he doesn't, he won't. Now go away. I have work to do."

I watch her arrange and rearrange those ledger books three times, as if they can't find a comfortable spot in a lumpy bed.

She finally looks at me. "Why are you still standing there?" she says. "I have nothing more to say to you. Get lost, Cantor."

I crush my smoke in the ashtray, keep my eyes on Abby, keep alive any hope that she gives a damn about Nick.

But she says nothing more. She's done with me. "Let me know if Sig gets in touch with you," I say on my way out the office door.

Out in the main room, the place is almost empty. The few remaining guys are tidying up, packing telephones, ledger books, and stacks of betting sheets in boxes. A big guy pushes the last of the furniture and other equipment out a back door to a loading dock where I guess a truck is waiting to take the stuff to a safe location, or maybe even dump it all in the river.

It wouldn't be the first time the East River has taken the apparatus of crime into its watery bosom. The river's been known to welcome crime's practitioners into its depths, too. Could be I'll end up there someday. Suits me. The company would sure be chummy.

By the time I get back to my Buick, I know something is very wrong in the triangle of Nick, Abby, and Sig. And I also know that there's a flashy red and black '57 Plymouth with gaudy chrome and pointy fins blocking my car. That's the last thing I know before there's a painful slam against the back of my head and everything in front of me—my Buick, the Plymouth, all of Front Street—spins in a whirlpool turning black.

Chapter Three

"My apologies, Cantor. The boys loused up." The guy's voice seeps through the mud clogging my brain. Slowly, the mud starts to dry up, bits of it crumbling away. My brain begins to function just enough to let me think a little, become aware of my body, which tells me I'm in a lumpy chair and that wherever the chair and I are has the throat-gagging stink of dirty bedsheets, stale tobacco, and old sweat.

"You want a drink, Cantor?" the voice says to me. The voice is familiar, a baritone with a certain warmth inside it.

Enough of the mud has finally crumbled away for my brain to command me to open my eyes.

I blink a lot. I have to, so that my eyes can work their way back into focus and to make sure I can believe what I finally see: Nick Fortunato standing in front of me.

Somewhere between the ache where I was slammed at the back of my head and the remaining mud still clinging to my brain, I'm relieved and I'm angry. My old friend isn't dead or even just bloodied; my old friend had me attacked and kidnapped.

He gives me the full-of-humor smile I've known for years, the smile of an almost honest used car salesman. It suits his almost handsome face: dark hair, easygoing brown eyes, movie-star chiseled features mucked up a bit by his imperfectly healed broken nose, the remnant of a Coney Island teenage brawl.

He's decked out in brown slacks, a white turtleneck pullover and a beige sports jacket with nubby brown flecks. Nick always was a smart dresser. That's another thing our friendship has in common: a taste for fine clothes.

We're not in his apartment. We're in a shadowy room with dull greenish walls. There's a portable TV on a rolling stand next to me, a small refrigerator and a hotplate in a corner, and a sagging bed behind Nick. Yellow neon light flashes on and off through the Venetian blinds in the single window, threatening to make my headache worse. Slats of the yellow light cut across the bed, revealing my overcoat and cap lumped like a dead body on the red chenille bedspread. The red chenille is old and dull as dried blood. I don't doubt for a minute that murders happened on that bed.

I have enough consciousness by now to realize that the flashing light comes from a sign hung outside on the building that says ROOMS.

We're in a cheap hotel.

I have a thousand questions, all of them starting with *What the hell . . .?* but the first thing out of my barely working mouth is, "Yeah, I'll take that drink, Nick."

"I brought along a bottle of Chivas," he says on his way to a decrepit bureau near the bed. The slats of flashing yellow light seem to tear at his face and claw at his fancy duds. It's a relief to my vision and my headache when he passes beyond the light and pours a couple of drinks from a bottle on the bureau. "I know better than to serve you cheap scotch," he says with an affable shrug. "After what you've been through, you deserve your favorite whiskey."

"Just what have I been through, Nick? That is, besides thinking you were injured or even dead after seeing blood on your living room carpet. And oh yeah, getting knocked out on Front Street and waking up in a fleabag hotel. Where the hell are we, anyway?"

He passes back through the slatted light, taking the bottle of Chivas with him, and hands me a scotch, neat, in a scratched bathroom glass. The shoddy glass doesn't matter. The good scotch clears the last of the mud from my brain. I see the shabby room, the flashing yellow light, and Nick more clearly now. Frankly, I miss the muddy blur.

Nick downs his drink, I down mine, too, and he pours us each another. Smiling, he spreads his arms wide, glass in hand. "Welcome to the luxe accommodations of the Cortland Hotel on the wrong end of West One-Hundred-and-I-Don't-Know-What Street in the Bronx. Safe haven for a man in hiding, courtesy of your friend and mine, Sig Loreale. And I really am sorry you got banged around, Cantor. Look, you and I go back a long ways. We know each other's heart and soul, so I figured when you didn't find me home you'd nose around down on Front Street. Honestly, I'm flattered that you gave enough of a damn to try to find out why I skipped our birthday bash."

I take another swig of the scotch, and wonder how far my friendship will extend in this mess Nick's tangled me up in. But after a glance at Nick, at the exhaustion and worry behind the familiar smile, I know the answer to that question: I'll take it all the way, because no other way matters.

"So sure, I sent my boys to Front Street," he says, "but I only told them to bring you here, not knock you out and kidnap you. The galoots got a helluva talking to when they brought you in. They were lucky that a talking to is all I gave them."

"I suppose you should hire a better class of galoot."

He gives that a sad snicker which tries but doesn't quite make it to a laugh. "They don't make 'em classy anymore," he says. "There aren't any honorable gangsters anymore, either. Loreale's the last of the breed."

"Sig? Honorable?" I'd laugh out loud, except my head still hurts. Best I can do is a smiling grunt. "Face it, Nick, Sig would have his mother killed if it suited his business interests. You're giving a lot of credit to a guy you're hiding from."

"You've got it all wrong, Cantor," he says, half frowning, half smiling. "Sig is the reason I'm still alive and that I'm safe here. Sig *needs* me alive. I'm one of his better investments. By protecting me, he's protecting his money."

I take another pull on my drink, but even the good whiskey can't cut through my confusion. Sig Loreale isn't the type to save anyone's life. He's better known for increasing the population of corpses.

"Look, Nick," I say with sigh, "I'm tired. My mind's spinning with too many threads and none of them tie together." I try to get comfortable in the lumpy chair, though it's a lost cause. I may as well be sitting on rocks. "So how about you tell me what's really going on. After all, I just got thumped on the head and kidnapped to this high-class resort, only to open my eyes and see a guy I was afraid might be dead. So yeah, I deserve an explanation. Oh, and by the way, happy birthday."

"Hah! Helluva birthday, yeah?" he says, and adds a shrug meant to convince us both that he's easy about whatever he's gotten himself into. He's not succeeding. His shoulders are tight as clenched fists. They look like they hurt.

He takes another swig of scotch, wipes his mouth with the back of his hand, then lets out a breath that wants to spew out every worry he's ever had. "Okay, then," he finally says, "here's the story. I had just set a couple of wine glasses on the coffee table when my doorbell rang. It was too soon for our birthday get-together, but I wasn't expecting anyone other than you, so I figured maybe you'd come early. When I opened the door, though, a guy I didn't know, a slender young guy, early twenties, maybe a little older, stood there with a big grin on his face and tufts of blond hair sticking out from under his hat. He looked more like those pictures you see of California surf bums than a New York sharpie. Maybe that's why he'd turned up the collar of his black overcoat tough-guy-style. I gave him a polite hello and asked who he was and what he wanted; you know, the 'May I help you?' bit and all that. Next thing I know, he pulls a gun on me, a big .45 rigged with a silencer. He sticks the gun in my belly, pushes me inside the living room, and tells me he's got a message for me from his employer."

Nick's pacing as he tells me all this. He suddenly stops and rubs the back of his neck, trying to release the tension that shoots from him like an electric charge. When he finally turns to face me, he's grinning. But it's not a happy grin. It's an angry one.

"And the message he gave me was a real corker," he says. "Get this, Cantor, the guy says he's here to give me a chance to clear out of my place on Front Street so that his boss's organization can move in and take over. Can you believe it? He says this to me, *me*, Nick Fortunato, Nicky Fast Hands, every gambler's favorite guy, the biggest bookie in town, in business with none other than Sig Loreale. So you know what I did? I laughed! That's what I did, laughed and told him to tell his boss to change plans before Loreale makes his own deadly plans for whoever sent the kid."

Despite my headache, despite my inside-out night, I gotta smile at Nick's chutzpah to laugh at a guy who has a gun aimed at his belly. That's the Coney Island in him, the wild, do-or-die-ride we both grew up with. "How'd he take the threat about Loreale?" I say.

"That's the crazy part," Nick says, flinging his arm for emphasis and nearly spilling his drink on his snazzy jacket. "It didn't faze the punk one bit. The SOB just laughed back and tells me that Sig's days are numbered, too. So I says to him, 'Listen, tell your boss—whoever the hell it is—to grow a pair of big ones before going after Loreale. And just who is this boss of yours, anyway?'"

"Did he come across with a name?"

"Nope. Said it's none of my concern, but that his boss figures it's time for the old geezer to move over. And then he says to me, 'And you're not getting any younger, either. I'm your replacement.' Well, that did it, Cantor. Hell, I'm nowhere near old. We're the same age, right? What are we, barely forty-ish?"

"Yeah," I say with a snicker of defiance and a shrug of resignation, "barely forty-ish." Okay, not old, but not kids anymore, either, which the lumpy chair's pummeling and pinching of my body reminds me.

"I've still got plenty of juice in me," Nick says. "So you know what? Gun or no gun, I slapped him so hard his eyes nearly popped outta his arrogant head. The punk's surprise gave me an opening to grab his gun, but he came back at me with a punch to the gut. Stupid kid, he didn't figure that when I was hunched over he couldn't see that I twisted the .45 right into his belly. A .45 slug makes a big hole."

That sits me up. "Then it's *his* blood I saw on your carpet?"

The last time I saw a look of tenderness on Nick's face was that time he saved my young life and got me away from those angry thugs on the street. "Oh man," he says, "oh man, I guess you must've thought the blood was mine."

"It crossed my mind, yeah."

He gives that a deep sigh, a slow, weight-of-the-world shake of his head, and says, "So instead of hosting an old friend, I end up with a dead shmegeg on my carpet."

"Which meant that Sig needed to know about it."

"Yeah. I figured real fast that Sig needs to know that someone is after him, so I phoned him, filled him in on what the kid said and told him that the kid was now lying dead on my living room carpet. He told me about this hotel, said he owns it, and to get here as fast as I can. He said he'd have his people take care of the body."

Uh-huh, there's nothing Sig hates more than loose ends, and a body lying around is the loosest of loose ends. I wonder if the punk is now at the bottom of the East River, along with Nick's bookie furniture. "The body was already gone by the time

I arrived," I say. "Did Sig say how long you'll have to stay here?"

"He didn't say, just told me to lay low until he tells me otherwise. You should've heard him, Cantor. You know how slow he talks and how cold each word sounds. Well, ice was forming on my phone."

I don't usually like keeping things from people I care about, but I decide to keep it to myself that I spoke to Sig, too, and that he warned me off. Nick doesn't need any more bad news. I only say, "Okay, just do as he says. You're probably pretty safe if you're under Sig's protection."

"What about you, Cantor? If I figured out that you'd nose around to find out what happened to me, you gotta figure that Sig will sniff it out, too. Maybe you should talk to him?"

"Could be," I say as I get up from the chair, giving away nothing.

I have to walk through the slashes of flashing yellow light to pick up my coat and cap from the bed. It's like walking through the gates of Hell.

"Listen, Nick, you need anything? Sandwiches or other stuff to eat? More booze?"

"Nah, I'm okay. I'm stocked for a few days. I doubt I'll be here any longer than that. But thanks anyway, Cantor. Hey, it's good to know we still have each other's backs."

"Always," I say, shaking his hand. "I'll be in touch, Nick."

He gives me a nod and pours himself another drink as I walk out the door.

He must've turned on the television, because I hear music and people laughing as I walk down the hall to the elevator. Sure, what else has Nick got to do besides get drunk and watch TV? I decide I'll drop by once in a while, keep him company. I don't care what Sig has to say about it.

The elevator arrives. Two of the hotel's white-shoe clientele get out as I step in: a threadbare rummy who smells like a urinal in a cheap saloon, and who can barely walk, and a dumpy Apple

Annie with tangled blond hair and disheveled clothes and whose rough life ate up her looks a long time ago, if she ever had them. The rummy gives me the shivers, and Apple Annie breaks my heart.

Outside on the street, I stand for a minute below the flashing ROOMS sign to get my bearings and figure which direction to find a subway. I don't know The Bronx too well. But the borough, like the rest of New York, is honeycombed with subway tunnels and station stops. If I keep walking I'll find a station sooner or later.

I'm about to walk toward the corner when I hear a crash of breaking glass and a gagged shout followed by a thud and a sickening crunch on the sidewalk.

In the harsh yellow light, Nick lies crumpled and broken on the pavement. Glass slivers in the rips of his snazzy white-and-brown flecked sports jacket sparkle a grisly, flashing neon yellow. Shards of glass glare red in the blood oozing from his crushed head. His eyes are open, catching the garish light. He's staring up at nothing until I kneel down over him, and then he's staring at me.

I'm caught in his stare, his dead stare that grabs me into its emptiness, a place where Nick feels nothing anymore but I feel sick and twisted with pain.

Much as I want to cradle the guy, cry over him, shout him back to life, and run back inside the hotel to try and find whoever pushed Nick out that window and beat the SOB to a pulp, I know deep in my outlaw marrow that I can't wait around for the inevitable arrival of the cops. It's not a good idea for me to be found with a dead body. Considering my lousy reputation with the cops, a dead body at my feet would get me locked up or even fried faster than an express subway train at rush hour.

Nick would understand. If he could he'd tell me to save myself, that this is no time for tears and crazy acts of loyalty. He'd tell me that I should just get the hell out of here.

He'd save my life again.

Chapter Four

I still feel rotten and sick at heart by the time I pick up my car on Front Street around ten-thirty and drive to Sig's place. If anything, the knot in my gut is tighter, the anger running through me is colder, and the memory of Nick lying smashed on the pavement has grown even sharper. My usual joy in the city, especially at night, when the town's millions of lights sparkle with greedy glamour, instead sits choked in my throat.

None of that is going to do me any good when I powwow with Sig. He'd only pick at those feelings and make them worse. Digging around in an adversary's pain is one of the ways he exerts control. So I bury my grief and anger as much as I can, push them down out of Sig's reach.

Sig lives like a lord in the penthouse of an office tower he owns on West Fortieth Street. The building's a streamlined skyscraper of black brick topped by a golden crown of arches on the wrap-around terrace. It's the perfect roost for the city's Lord of Crime. He can look out from his terrace to see the vast city whose rackets and politicians and cops he controls. When he looks down, he can see the city's people, tiny as insects, who have no idea that he picks their pockets every day, taking a dime here, a dollar there, every time they have their trash picked up, or buy a cup of coffee, a hat, a bag of groceries, or have a drink at a nightclub or bar. He even picks the teenage pockets of the kids buying the records of the latest rock-'n'-roll heartthrob.

It's getting late, almost eleven, and maybe most guys Sig's age—I figure him creeping past seventy, if he isn't already there—would be tucked up in bed by now. But I'm sure Sig is still up and pulling the city's strings. I'm sure because he had to arrange the retrieval and likely disposal of the dead kid in Nick's apartment, and because of what Nick told him, what the kid said about muscling Sig out, but most of all because I'm absolutely sure he's already heard about Nick's plunge to the pavement. I'm sure because the cops are probably on the scene by now and Sig knows every move the cops make.

Since it's after the workday, the door to the building is locked, the day-to-day business people and office help having all gone home hours ago. I ring the night bell to call the night watchman, smoke a cigarette and watch the goings-on on Fortieth Street while I wait. Despite the hour, and this being Manhattan, the street is still busy with people coming from the nearby theaters or on their way to the late shows at nightclubs. Men hold onto their hats in the chill November wind. Women, some in furs, some in wool coats in lively colors, hold their gloved hands around their collars and tuck them closer to their necks. Slender, exotic turbans and broad-brimmed picture-hats are the fashionable styles for women this year, and I like them. Then again, I enjoy most things women do, like the seductive click of their high heels along the pavement.

The big bronze-and-glass entry door to Sig's building opens, breaking off my musings of the street. The night watchman's a dry-faced, gray-haired guy in a faded blue workman's outfit. His name's Gus Balchuk, and he's been the night watchman here for a year or so after the previous night watchman annoyed Sig for some reason and was never seen or heard from again.

Gus gives me the once-over he always gives me when I

show up here, making it clear he thinks my choice of clothing is something his bible wouldn't countenance, but since I'm a friend of his boss he figures it's none of his concern.

He says, "Evenin', Cantor. I guess you're here to see Mr. Loreale. Seems a funny hour for him to be entertaining, but who am I to question what the boss does?"

"Entertaining?"

"Well, you ain't the first one to come by. I'll have to call him, let him know you're here before I can let you up."

I follow Gus across the huge lobby, a shadowy, black tile cathedral lit after hours only by wall sconces. The meager light gives the place a funereal feel, which I suppose is an appropriate setting for the murderous guy who plots and plans upstairs in his penthouse.

We arrive at a bank of elevators, three of them for the daily business tenants, and the fourth, at the far end, a private car only for Sig's penthouse. Gus picks up the intercom next to Sig's elevator. When the call's answered, likely by one of Sig's stable of bodyguards, Gus says, "Sorry to bother ya, but Cantor Gold is here to see Mr. Loreale." After a moment, he nods, says, "Yeah, okay," and hangs up. He takes a key from the ring dangling from his belt and unlocks the elevator.

All during the ride up to the penthouse, I keep thinking about what Gus said: that Sig is entertaining. Who the hell else is up there at this time of night? And why would Gus think that Sig, a dour and solitary guy who'd probably never even attended a social gathering in his life, never mind hosted one, would entertain anybody?

I'm still chewing on this when the elevator arrives at the penthouse. Sig's place occupies the entire floor. His door is already open. One of Sig's thugs, a lump of a guy who goes by the moniker Bensonhurst Benny, because that's the Brooklyn neighborhood he comes from, stands in the doorway, a galoot in a badly fitting black suit.

He gives me a smile which has all the charm of an annoyed hippopotamus. "They're in the den," he says. "Now hand it over."

He doesn't have to say what he wants me to hand over.

I have a lousy choice. I can either hand over my gun without argument, or let Benny frisk me. I opt for the former. Having the hippo's paws on me would further ruin my already lousy night. So I hand him my gun and top it off by giving him my coat and cap, too. He's not pleased at being treated like a coat-check girl.

I have to pass through the living room to get to the den. The room's full of memories, some good, some rough. The best are tied up with the paintings and other artifacts I've acquired for Sig over the years, often heisting them from museums or fancy houses in various parts of the world, whose owners had no intention of giving their treasures up. Sig is particularly fond of eighteenth- and nineteenth-century landscapes, the kind depicting vast aristocratic estates with peasants tending to the land and the manor. It's how Sig interprets the world: the little people in service to guys like him, the guys who own or run everything.

I knock on the door to the den, soon hear Sig's slow and gravelly, "Come in, Cantor."

Inside, Sig is sitting behind his desk, a sleek but substantial hunk of burled maple. It's the kind of furniture that quietly advertises the power of the man sitting behind it. The stuff on his desk—a hefty brass lighter, a globular crystal ashtray, a bronze goose-neck desk lamp—are additional props in this theater of power.

Sig's usual attire of dark suits, crisp white shirts, and dark ties, is another testament to his position at the top of the power heap. Tonight, though, at this late hour, he's wearing a robe, red silk with a black satin shawl collar that eerily catches the light of the desk lamp. I guess I disturbed his bedtime plans after all.

The rest of him is mostly in shadow, except where the lamplight finds the more imposing parts of his face: his fleshy lips, heavy jowls, the bags under his heavy-lidded eyes, and the sharp glint in his dark pupils.

I'm not surprised by any of that. I've seen Sig in the darkness of his wood-paneled study lots of times. But I'm nearly knocked back on my heels at the sight of who's sitting in one of the two gray leather club chairs opposite Sig's desk, her wine-smooth, "Hello, Cantor," as alluring now as it was a few hours ago in her office in Nick's bookie parlor.

Sig's, "Sit down, Cantor," isn't alluring at all. It's a command.

I sit down in the other club chair. "I guess I don't have to explain why I'm here," I say. "Looks like you're already a few steps ahead of me, as always, Sig. Okay then, so what are you going to do about what happened to Nick? And please don't give me that song-and-dance about staying out of it. Like it or not, I'm already in it. The blood in Nick's apartment put me in it. Nick sailing out the window of that crummy hotel where you stashed him put me even deeper in it, especially since he nearly landed on my head. And we both know, Sig, that Nick's trip to the pavement wasn't voluntary."

Sig folds his hands on his desk, lowers his head for a moment, then looks up again and straight at me. There's no expression on his face. Absolutely none.

Every muscle and bone in my body wants to cringe.

"Cantor," he finally says, taking his time with my name, "someone, someone very foolish but very sharp, has invaded my operation. I am not happy about that. Whoever they are will be taught a lesson when I find them. And I will find them." The glint in his eyes is almost hidden when his eyelids slide down, leaving only slits, ice cold slits of calculation and vengeance. When he looks up again, the vengeance is gone but the annoyance remains. "And I am not happy about having to tell you again to stay out of it. The unfortunate death of Mr. Fortunato only complicates—"

"*Unfortunate?*" I practically bark it, my calm broken by Sig's cold-heartedness. "Is that all Nick's murder is to you? An unfortunate complication? Nick played straight with you for years, Sig. He never held back a penny. He stayed loyal to you, not because you could threaten him but because he honored his commitments. That's the kind of guy he was, and the best you can come up with about his murder is *unfortunate*? Y'know, I don't care if you like it or not, Sig, but I'm staying in this every step of the way. And if I find whoever killed Nick before you do, I'll do something about it, because Nick Fortunato mattered to me. You wouldn't understand, Sig, because nobody matters to you anymore."

He hasn't taken his eyes off me, only now his expression isn't entirely blank. There's a small furrow in his brow, a slight narrowing of his eyes. If I didn't know better, I'd say he looks disappointed. But I do know better.

I hear Abby's soft and buttery, "Cantor," and feel her hand on my arm. She's turned toward me, leaning just enough over the arm of the club chair for a bit of light from the desk lamp to fall on her pale blue pullover sweater, reminding me again of just how well she fills it. "Listen to me," she says. "Sig is right. It would be better if you stayed away from all this." The smile she gives me, feminine and worldly to her core, would ordinarily trigger delectable imaginings of the decidedly erotic sort. To tell the truth, those thoughts creep up on me now. But at this moment, in this room, Abby's smile and her unexpected presence incite more curiosity than lust.

I peel her hand from my arm, give her palm a departing kiss before dropping her hand back in her lap. It seems to amuse her.

I need a minute to work my way through all the threads Sig and Abby are spinning around me, so I take my pack of Chesterfields and my lighter from my inside suit jacket pocket, take a smoke out for myself, light it and offer one to Abby, who slides one out from the pack. As I light it for her, I decide which thread to pull. "Tell me, Abby, just where do you come in? The corpse of your recent employer is barely cold in the morgue, and you already have Sig's ear and—what? His trust? Don't fool yourself, kiddo."

Maybe I've hit a nerve, because she looks away from me and hides for a moment behind an exhale of smoke. When she turns to look at me again, whatever nerve I've hit seems to have settled back down. She's as sleek and serene as a cat in the sun. I wouldn't be surprised if she purred. "Do I have *your* trust?" she says.

It's my turn to smile, though it's a chilly one. "Do you need it?"

"Let's say I'd like it."

"Then I have to know why. You don't get something for nothing. You've been in the game long enough, Abby, to know that by now. Hell, even your new pal, Sig Loreale, knows that."

Sig's gruff, "That's enough, Cantor," takes over with the force of a fist. "I advise you again to stay away from anything having to do with Mr. Fortunato and his death."

"Advised? Or warned, Sig?"

He takes a cigar from the humidor on his desk, lights it with the brass lighter beside it. The flame writhes obscenely with his breath. The tip of the cigar glows red, throwing the glow along his red robe and spreading slowly up his face. It's the stuff of nightmares. "Good night, Cantor," he says, flicking me away as indifferently as flicking cigar ash into an ashtray. "You may collect your gun at the door."

The neon-tinged midnight darkness of my living room, along with a tumbler of Chivas, takes the chill off the memory of that strange meeting in Sig's office. The scotch also helps me think, helps me figure my next move. There are people I should talk to, people who knew Nick or did business with him or placed bets with him. Among all those people, someone might have a line on who planned to move in on him, who might have wanted him dead, and has the guts—and the stupidity—to try to muscle Sig out of the way. This last thought gives me chuckle, a dark, sharp-edged chuckle, because whoever it is who's trying to get rid of Sig doesn't realize that as Sig Loreale gets older he's not getting weaker. He's getting even smarter, cagier, more patient, more dangerous.

I'm not getting any younger either. Sure, Sig's got a few decades on me, but as Nick reminded me, I'm no kid anymore. If I'm lucky, I'll pick up some of Sig's smarts and patience along the road to my dotage. I'll need them.

The buzz at my door rescues me from thinking about Father Time nipping at my heels. It also interrupts the quiet pleasure of my scotch sipped slowly in the neon night in my living room. But most of all, it raises the hair on the back of my neck, because if a killer was clever enough to find Nick at the Cortland Hotel, they could be clever enough to find me.

I have my .38 in my hand when I open the door.

Laughing quietly at the sight of the gun and then smiling at me, Abby says, "I thought you liked me, Cantor."

Chapter Five

If Abby's arrival is a surprise, her entrance is downright memorable. She slides past me in the doorway with the smoothness of silk sliding along a leg.

"At least offer me a drink," she says. She stops while she's still in the entry hall and looks back at me with a hint of surprised disappointment. "Come on, Cantor. Surely you know how. Where's that chivalry of yours I've heard so much about?"

I catch on. I'm tempted to give her a slight bow just for a laugh, but I ditch that idea in favor of something I like better. I come around to face her, and unbutton the top button of her black cashmere coat. "May I?"

Her black-gloved hand pushes mine away before she slowly works her fingers down the line of red buttons. I can't help thinking that if she ever gets tired of the bookie racket she'd have a swell future as a stripper.

She smiles at me through this entire operation. It's the sort of smile that makes me want to ditch all that chivalry I'm supposed to have and just be a gorilla.

But chivalry wins out. When she's finished with the buttons and turns around, I help her off with her coat. It slides off her shoulders the way a coat should slide off a woman's shoulders, caressing her all the way down her arms.

I toss the coat over the hall chair then follow Abby into the living room and turn on a lamp next to the couch. The lamplight puts Abby in silhouette, a shadow of a woman who's here and not here at the same time.

She emerges again in flesh and bone when the lamplight fully finds her as she sits down on the couch. She's still wearing the pale blue pullover sweater, slender brown skirt, and that wide black leather belt that surrounds her waist like a lover's arm.

"Scotch?" I offer.

"Whatever you're having."

I pour her a tumbler of Chivas, refresh my own, and sit down again in my club chair, facing Abby.

She raises her glass in silent toast and takes a sip of the scotch, leaving a seductive smear of red lipstick on the glass.

I take a deep swallow of my own drink, keep my eyes on Abby, who keeps her eyes on me. We're sizing each other up like two feral cats in an alley.

"Did Sig send you?" I say. "Does he think you can convince me to back off better than he can?"

She leans back into the couch, the cushions molding around her as if they enjoy the feel of her. "No, Sig didn't send me," she says. "I didn't tell him I was coming here, so I have no idea if he thinks I can do a better job of convincing you to back off. But yes, that's why I'm here. Please, you've got to listen to me, Cantor."

"It won't work, Abby."

"It has to."

"Why? What's in it for you? And what's the story of your arrangement with Sig? You're playing with fire, Abby. If Sig wants to, he'll burn you to ash."

It's the first time I see something other than confidence in her eyes. A glimmer of unease creeps into the smolder. But after another swallow of her drink, she says, "I can handle Sig."

I can't avoid a sneer, even a light and humorous one. "I have no doubt that all you have to do is crook your little finger and you can control any man—and several women," I add with a slightly libidinous smile—"who look at you, and even those who don't. But Sig Loreale is another matter."

"He's still a man," she says. Her voice strokes the word *man* as if petting an obedient dog.

"Sig's male," I say. "But a man? That implies he's human. There's disagreement about that among people who've either trusted him or tangled with him. So I ask you again, Abby, what's your business with him? Are you really angling to take over Nick's bookie operation?"

"What if I am?" She gives that an easygoing shrug of defiance. "No one knows Nick's operation better than I do. And I'm the one who made sure Sig's payoffs were on the up-and-up, on time and to the dime. That should count for something."

"So you figure Sig owes you, and you want him to finance your takeover. Listen, Abby, do you really want Sig Loreale to be the guy behind the curtain? The guy who controls every dollar you take in and pay out? He'll be breathing down your neck like a dragon with fire in his nostrils."

She waves that away, says, "You worry too much," through a smile that's equal parts amused by me and feeling sorry for me. The amused part looks over the rim of her glass as she takes another sip of her drink. After swallowing the whiskey, she says, almost cooing it, "You really are charming, Cantor, but your worry is pointless. Sig has no reason not to trust me. And besides, he never crowded Nick, never interfered with the way Nick ran the business. As long as Sig got his cut, he left Nick alone. It's true, my relationship with Sig won't be the same as Nick's. How can it be?" she adds with a wink. "But he'll always get a cut." I've always thought of Abby as sharp, a woman who knows her way around, knows what's what and won't be played for a fool. But right now I want to take Abby by her perfect shoulders and shake her out of her delusion that she can handle Sig Loreale.

Instead, chivalry—or at least the good sense not to do something that would anger her—takes over again. I just take a deep swallow of my scotch, let the whiskey calm me, keep me in my chair. If I can't shake her up bodily, maybe words will do the trick to keep her safe. "You don't get it, Abby. You'll never be able to. Listen to me, Sig left Nick alone because Nick and Sig—and me, too, if you must know—the three of us go back a long way, since Nick and I were kids in Coney Island and Sig was taking over the Coney rackets. He used to read us the riot act about getting in his way. We learned not to cross him, and he kept an eye on us as we grew up and moved into rackets of our own. That kind of history is the balance wheel that made it all work over the years, and kept it working. But your history with Sig is newer, and colder. It's just business, and maybe not even that. You might've been the day-to-day brains running Nick's bookie operation, Abby, but believe me, to Sig you were simply the hired help."

She doesn't like the description. She gives me a look meant to shrivel me. "If you're trying to scare me, Cantor, you're doing a lousy job."

"Then what can I do to scare you? What can I do to make sure you're not the next one tossed out a window?"

It didn't work. She's not scared at all. She just gives that a dismissive smile. "You're sweet, Cantor," she says, her tone smooth and sultry. "But Sig didn't kill Nick."

"Okay, probably not," I say, shrugging. "But let's say it's a good bet that whoever tossed Nick is either the fool who's trying to muscle Sig out of the way, or someone who works for the fool. And if you're in league with Sig now, that same fool won't hesitate to come after you. Don't you get it that I'm trying to save your life, Abby?"

She's as serene at the idea that her life might be in danger as if I'd just told her a boring joke. She simply slides her shoes off, a pair of black leather numbers with stiletto heels that could double as ice picks or murder weapons, then stretches her legs across the couch. Through her sheer hosiery I can see that her toenails are painted the same red as her fingernails, which is the same red as her lipstick. I'm looking at three stops on a map of a vacation my libido wouldn't mind taking. "My, my," she purrs, "trying to save my life? This is how I like you, Cantor. More of that chivalry you're famous for. Is that how you got those scars on your face? You know, they give you a certain swashbuckling allure. That little curved one over your right eye is particularly dashing."

"I'm not trying to be chivalrous. I'm just trying to find out what the hell is going on. Why does Sig want me out of the picture? Why do you? What's going on with you, Abby?"

"Oh, please," she says with a toss of her head and the kind of small laugh that scolds. "Don't be dull, Cantor. It doesn't suit you. What's going on with me is the same thing that goes on with you."

"Is that so? You'll have to enlighten me. I'm afraid I don't share your warm feelings for Mr. Loreale."

She sits up on the couch, lamplight catching the sheen on the soft waves of her dark hair, the creaminess of her red lipstick, the shape of her beneath her sweater. These are sights I could get lost in, let my mind wander into delicious daydreams. But the life-and-death antics the night has thrown at me force my attention away from Abby's body and to her words. "It doesn't matter how you feel about Sig," she says, "or even how I feel about him, for that matter. You and I live in the same world, Cantor. The same world as Sig Loreale." She lifts her glass toward me. "My drink needs refreshing. Do you mind?"

I refresh both our drinks, sit down again in my chair, take a pull on the Chivas and let the whiskey sharpen my thoughts. "Sure, we're in the same world," I say, "but we're in it for different reasons. For you, it's a way to make a good living. It's tough for women to get ahead in the legit world. And with your head for numbers, the bookmaking racket is perfect for you. Sig, though, he's in it for the power, the control, the iron grip he has on every racket, every politician, every big business big shot, and every dollar in town. The money that comes with that control, and a willingness to kill, helps him keep that grip. He's a dangerous SOB, Abby. You know it as well as I do."

She gives that a slow nod, her eyes closed for a moment, lost in thoughts I'm not privy to. "I've been handling dangerous men all my life, Cantor," she finally says, her eyes open now but not looking at me. When she does look at me again, whatever those thoughts were, whatever dark memories they took her to, are gone. She's the slightly amused enchantress once more. "What about you, Cantor? You're an art thief. You know all about paintings. You even know the business of art. Why don't you just work in a museum? Or make big money at an art gallery. Some of the new abstract paintings go for fistfuls of cash."

It's my turn to laugh, a snicker filled with the rebellion that's sustained me for years. "Why do I steal art instead of doing legit business with it? Because I have a better chance of staying out of jail as a thief than living in the legitimate world. You look surprised."

"Well, yes, I suppose I am. I've heard that the art game can be cutthroat, but I didn't think jail figured into it."

"I'm not talking about the art game. I'm talking about how the Law and the society that lives by it pegs me a criminal just because of who I take to dinner, who I dance with, who I bed. If a cop catches me even holding hands with a woman, or if he just wants to give me a hard time about the clothes I wear—"

"Which you wear rather well, Cantor."

I like the way she says it, and the teasing look that comes with it, but Abby's still a mystery, a potentially dangerous one, so I just go on filling her in on my risky life. "That cop would be tickled pink to clap the steel cuffs on me, and the Law would be quick to send me to the slammer or the loony bin. So I don't owe the Law a thing, Abby, least of all a law-abiding life."

She stretches herself along the couch again, her smile more knowing than sympathetic, a smile that has the goods on me. "Oh, but you love it, Cantor. You love the outlaw life."

I can't deny it. I won't even try. Ignoring the Law and kicking sand in its face when I can gives me a freedom the straight-backs who own the Law would never understand. And it's given me money, plenty of money, the kind of money it takes to keep myself in new cars, custom-tailored suits, and a first-rate lawyer who gets me out of scrapes and knows how to beat the Law at its own game.

So my grin's full of pleasure when I say, "Sure, I love it." But the grin fades as I get back to the reality Abby's ignoring. "I'd love it a whole lot more if I knew what's cooking between you and Sig. You want him to do business with him? Okay, but that hasn't got a thing to do with why both of you want me to get lost when it comes to finding out who killed Nick. So tell me what the hell is going on, Abby, or get out."

She didn't expect that, and frankly neither did I. But I'm tired of the runaround she and Sig are giving me. And I'm tired of the betrayals the two of them find so easy to do: Sig not caring about the murder of a guy he's known since childhood, and Abby doing deals with Sig before Nick's even had a decent funeral.

So the hell with them. I'll arrange Nick's funeral, and I'll do what I have to do to find out who killed him. I owe it to him. I owe it to our childhood and how we survived it. I owe it to a friendship better than I deserved.

My outburst hasn't turned a hair on Abby's head or stiffened a muscle in her luscious body. She sits up on the couch smooth and easy, slips her feet back into her shoes, and swallows the last of her drink before getting up. "I tried, Cantor. Really, I tried to warn you. You said you're trying to save my life. You have it backwards. I came here to try to save yours."

"I didn't know you cared," I say as I follow her to the door.

She picks up her coat and gloves from the hall chair, slides into the coat and slips on the gloves. Her hand is on the doorknob when she says over her shoulder, "There's a lot you don't know, Cantor. There's a lot you're better off not knowing."

Chapter Six

Judson Zane, my right-hand guy, my walking encyclopedia, telephone book, and record-keeper all rolled into one, is as adorable as he is smart. At least, the town's debs think so. I pulled Judson out of a teenage street gang about twelve years ago, figured a skinny kid with wire-rimmed glasses who could survive the streets by sensing all the angles was a kid who had potential. My business was growing at the time, and I needed a smart head to keep the nitty gritty details straight. Judson's been keeping everything tight and tidy ever since.

It's well past midnight when I phone him, but he's a guy still young enough to be awake and enjoying one of the debs he attracts like ants to a picnic, or he's asleep and young enough to handle interrupted slumber. "It's me, Judson," I say after his hello.

I hear music in the background, a song with a couple of guys—they sound even younger than Judson—singing a jukebox tune in close harmony, something about all they have to do is dream. Then I hear a young girl somewhere in the room say, "Don't be long, Judson, honey," her voice in that youthful moment between naïve purring and experienced teasing.

Memories crawl up on me.

Judson says, "Oh, hello, Cantor." He's all business now. "I wondered when I'd hear from you. I heard about Nick Fortunato, figured you'd be getting into it." Nothing gets by my young genius. "What do you need?" he says.

"I need the home addresses of four people who worked for Nick: Freddie Holmes, Mike Landers, Chickie D'Andrea, and Abby O'Neill."

"I assume they're not in the book."

"You assume right. Same reason we're not in the book."

"You home?"

"Yeah, but not for long. I'll check back with you in the morning."

New York is great for finding anything you want, any time you want, day or night. Right now, after a night I can only classify as teetering between miserable and terrifying, what I need is comfort, comfort that soothes pain, soothes a heart breaking over the murder of a good friend, the kind of comfort I find in a woman's arms, preferably accompanied by a stiff drink. Which is why I'm at the bar of the Green Door Club, a little hideaway in an alley just off Fourteenth Street. I'm enjoying a scotch poured by Peg Monroe, a bartender with brown skin, tender brown eyes, a hefty build, a Georgia drawl, and who I trust with my life and the drunken sob stories that occasionally come with it. Peg's been the barkeep here as long as I've been a patron, keeping everyone happy and keeping our secrets. She's the linchpin that keeps the place humming, and when necessary, during police raids for instance, or other bullying attempts by the Law, has kept various patrons safe, including me. There's a lot more to the Green Door Club than just a dance floor, and a lot more to Peg than just a bar.

Peg's not afraid of much, not even of the bigots who hate

anyone whose skin isn't white or whose dating habits aren't boy-gets-girl. And if she is afraid of them, her backbone of pride keeps her from showing it. So when it comes to my own insistence on having a place in a world that hates me, too, I've learned a thing or two from Peg.

Though Peg's been the solid center of the Green Door Club, there have been lots of changes over the years. For instance, there used to be a bandstand with an all girl band playing ballroom tunes, Broadway show tunes, and even a bit of jazz. There's just a jukebox now, a chrome and red-and-aqua-enameled steel behemoth where the small bandstand used to be. The tunes booming through its speakers are mostly rock-'n'-roll and teenage ballads, like the one I heard through Judson's phone. The music's a little noisy for my not-so-young taste, but that's okay. There's pleasure to be had watching the new mix of younger women from all over the city move their bodies with their rock-'n'-roll energy and pizzazz, even now at nearly one o'clock in the morning.

The décor of the club's changed, too. The booths used to be red leather, now they're aqua vinyl. Very modern, very jukebox-y. And just a few years ago there were small, shaded lamps on the tables in the booths, as well as on the tables around the dance floor, and along the walls. The pretty light sent a soft glow through the room, highlighting a colorful dress here, a snappy dinner jacket there. These days, the lights on the tables and around the walls are just sleek white plastic cylinders throwing a shadowy, Space Age sheen on pastel button-down sweaters, rolled-up blue jeans, denim or leather jackets, and the occasional colorful taffeta dress or sports jacket and tie.

Perusing the crowd, I take a little comfort in seeing that I'm not alone with my memories, that there's still a few of us around who remember the elegant days of chiffon-draped femmes and their evening-suited escorts, people like the interesting blonde two barstools from me. She's in a strapless pink satin cocktail dress, a form-fitting number you might see on a nightclub torch-song chanteuse, the satin glowing through the shadowy room and cigarette smoke. The dress fits the blonde like skin and reveals enough of her real skin at the bodice to invite ogling. Her hair is short, with that windblown look that tempts me to run my fingers through it whether she asks me to or not. Her profile, which is all I can see of her from my spot along the bar, is as refined as that of a princess. A naughty princess. She sips her martini with the ease of a practiced elbow and what appears to be appreciation of Peg's skill at mixing the perfect cocktail.

Peg gives me a cagey smile, the sort that usually accompanies an amiable clap on the back. "Waiting to make your move, Slick?" She's called me Slick for years. I don't mind. It suits me sometimes. With any luck, it'll suit me now.

I get up from my barstool, make my way to the blonde. "Hello," I say with a smile that's respectful but open to other developments. "Your martini's almost down to the olive. I'd love to buy you another. My name's Cantor, by the way."

"Yes, you're Cantor Gold. I knew who you were the minute you walked in." She's turned to look at me when she says it, and I see the full naughty-princess lure of her: come-to-me gray eyes, high cheekbones softly curved by creamy flesh, a mouth ripe for pleasure and whose dark pink lipstick would leave smears of satisfaction.

That's what I see. I have no doubt, though, that what she sees on my face is surprise. "You know me?" I say. "Have we met before? I can't imagine I'd ever forget you."

"No, we've never met," she says with offhand ease. "I've heard of you, though. And that small knife-shaped scar above your lip gives you away. Everyone knows how you got it."

This is getting interesting. "Is that so? And just who is *everyone*?"

"Oh, you know; the better nighttime circles, you might say. And the not so good circles, either." This comes on a laugh that's deep and sly. "Your name gets around." She runs a fingertip around the rim of her martini glass, creating a low, bell-like hum that somehow cuts through the thump of rock-'n'-roll on the jukebox. Or maybe I'm just in tune with every move she makes. "They know the name Cantor Gold as far away as Chicago," she says.

I don't know whether to be flattered, intrigued, or worried. The kind of people I know in Chicago might sing my praises or want me dead. "Chicago," I say, letting the word go nowhere in particular while I let the conversation go wherever she wants it to go, and wondering if the conversation could go to places I don't want it to. Dangerous places.

Her smile is friendly enough, though. "Born and raised in the Windy City," she says. "Pleased to finally meet you, Cantor Gold. My name's Lily Vardanian. And yes, you may buy me another martini,"

Her name has an unexpected warming effect on me, the warmth of recognition tinged with a searing edge. Lily Vardanian. A name I've heard said with respect among my circle of acquaintances, associates, even enemies. She's one of the best dips in the business. She can pick a pocket, a handbag, a suitcase, with fingers so feathery the mark feels nothing but air. What's more, the cops and the Feds don't bother coming after her anymore. Why? Because they use her to swipe papers from the desks, briefcases, file drawers, even the pants of big shots or foreign agents, likely when she's kissing their owners. The Feds originally asked her to train their spies in the art of delicate swiping in exchange for leaving her alone for her private activities, but she's too smart to reveal her professional secrets. She told them she'd do their sneak-jobs herself or it was no deal. They took the deal. J. Edgar Hoover hates her because he can't arrest her. Hell, he'd hate her, anyway.

"Well, well, it seems I'm in the presence of royalty," I say, and signal Peg to bring us fresh drinks. "Pleased and honored to finally meet you, too, Lily Vardanian. But if you knew who I was when I came in, why didn't you introduce yourself?"

"Because I thought it would be more fun to let you make the first move."

"Fun for who?" I say.

"Fun for both of us."

I like the way she says it. I like the way I feel about it.

"What brings you to New York?" I say.

"You know better than to ask questions, Cantor."

Yeah, I know better. And I'm probably better off not knowing the answers. I'd like the evening to move into less professional territory.

A slow song finally plays on the juke, a pretty tune, "You Send Me," by Sam Cooke, one of the newer crooners I like. I share his sentiments: Lily Vardanian absolutely sends me.

I'm about to ask her to dance, every inch of me looking forward to feeling her body against me, when she says, "Isn't that beautiful?" with a nod to the couples swaying on the dance floor. "Those blue jean'd butchy kids are adorable, aren't they? Holding their young ladies so tenderly. Like chivalrous knights, or gallant boys. I wonder how many of them wish they were, or could be. Well, maybe some will try." Looking at me, smiling an intriguing smile as she takes me in from head to toe and fingering the lapel of my suit, she says, "Have you ever thought about it, Cantor?"

"You mean go under the knife? A few people I know are thinking about it," I say. "It's still a tricky business. Takes guts, cash, and a trip to Europe. As for me, I'm content as is. What you see is what I am."

Lily raises her hand to my face, strokes the curved scar above my right eye. "Whatever you are, Cantor Gold, you're a work of art."

I've been called many things, some of them complimentary, some of them too crummy to repeat, but no one's ever flattered me by calling me a work of art. "Miss Vardanian," I say in my most courtly manner, "would you care to dance?"

Her laugh is low and dark with the lure of risky pleasure. "Are you sure you want me so close to you? You might be checking for your wallet every two minutes."

"I'll take my chances," I say.

She takes the olive from her martini, holds it between her lips for a moment before biting it in half and swallowing it. She finishes with a soft and satisfied, "Mmm," then says, "Why waste time dancing?"

Her hotel isn't far, one of those small but elegant places near Madison Square catering to guests who have money and taste and prefer to breeze in and out of town quietly.

Lily's room is on the second floor, a distance from the elevator but near the stairwell. It's the sort of setup I arrange when I travel and check into a hotel. Lily didn't tell me why she's in New York, but the setup tells me she's on a job. A job that's none of my business.

She turns the bedside lamp on when we walk into her room. The room's outfitted with comfortable furnishings and a big bed covered in pale green satin. She removes her white cashmere coat, casually throwing the expensive garment onto a chair as if tossing any old rag from her closet.

The lamplight picks up the high sheen of her blond hair. I don't wait for an invitation, I take hold of her and run my fingers through the golden strands.

The light also sends a glow along her satin dress, and I let my hands trace the line of light down her body. When she doesn't stop me, I let my hands roam her other places, creamy places above the bodice of her dress. The warmth of life radiates from her skin and into my fingers, life I need to feel to soothe the pain eating at me over Nick's death, over leaving his body smashed on the sidewalk.

Looking at me with sudden tenderness, Lily traces the scars on my face with her fingertip, starting with the small knife-shaped scar above my upper lip, then slides to the little slice at the corner of my mouth. As she glides her fingertip down to the straight line on my chin and then up to the jagged slash along my left cheek and finally back to the small curved number above my right eye, she gives a little "Mmm," and a whispery, "Your life is written in these scars. Maybe that's why I find them strangely attractive. And those threads of gray in your hair add a bit of worldly-wise seasoning. ."

Her touch ignites my lust for life again. By the time she pulls my hand around to the zipper along the back of her dress, I'm all hers, flesh, bone, and soul. As I slowly pull the zipper down, she lifts her face to mine and kisses me.

It's a confident kiss, a demanding kiss, the kind that insists I give in.

I start by sliding her dress off.

The next hours until dawn are filled with sexual demands made by each of us; what Lily wants of me for her pleasure, and what I need from her for mine. Sometimes it's a battle. Sometimes it's a surrender. But it's the stuff of life. It's our outlaw lives expressed as lust.

Chapter Seven

The morning sun's coming through my living room window by the time I arrive back at my apartment. It's an autumn sun, a cozy sun, a sun that tempts me to curl up in my big red chair with a cup of hot coffee and let my muscles unwind from the wild night that started with the scary business of Nick's disappearance, followed by the horror of his murder, and ended with the body to body ecstasy of Lily Vardanian. Every inch of my flesh will hold the memory of everything Lily and I did, all the gentleness and the savagery, and how it all felt. I don't know how long she'll be in town, but I know I want to see her again. I have to see her again. My flesh and most of my soul insist on it.

But the rest of my soul calls out to Nick. I can't let his murder twist in an unresolved limbo. A shower restores my sense of who I am and what I must do. Back in my bedroom, I reach for a pale yellow cotton shirt in the bureau drawer, but pull my hand back fast. The yellow fires up memories of that ugly yellow neon sign and Nick dead and bleeding under it.

I take out a pastel green shirt instead, match it up with a dark green tie with a tan chevron pattern, and a chocolate brown silk suit finished off with a pale green pocket square. Dressing well in a custom tailored suit is my daily declaration of insisting on having my place in a world that wishes I didn't. My .38 in its shoulder rig clinches it.

I phone Judson. He gives me the addresses I asked for.

Twenty minutes later, I'm driving down to the same downtown dockside neighborhood where Nick had his betting parlor. I park on Pearl Street, a couple of blocks from Nick's bookie joint. It's a shabby street of small warehouses, a few tenements, and a few stores selling rope and tools and other hardware for the maritime trade. At the corner is the inevitable saloon. Empty liquor and beer bottles roll around and clang in the gutter.

Mike Landers's place is in the middle of the block, a soot-stained tenement that's hosted fifty-odd years of sailors, dockside prostitutes, longshoremen whose pay is regularly shorted by their mobbed-up union, and families right off whatever boat brought them from whatever country they ran from in desperation and fear. The building is easy to get into. I don't even need the lockpicks I always carry with me. The lock's busted.

Mike's apartment is on the third floor. The stairs creak as I walk up. Radios play competing music from the thin-walled apartments, with blasts of rock-'n'-roll's amped-up electric guitars winning the noise battle over wailing babies, breaking chinaware, and the curses of angry tenants. The hall smells sour, like vinegar and cabbage and sweat.

Beats me why Mike would live in such a dump. I figure he made good dough as the chief of Nick's telephone crew. I can't picture Nick as a cheapskate employer. He wasn't that kind of guy. But then again, I didn't picture that he'd wind up dead on his birthday.

It takes Mike a minute to answer the door after my knock. When he does, he opens the door mere inches. His thin face is flushed and sweaty, his cheeks hollow as a couple of caves.

His brown hair is disheveled, and his bloodshot eyes are heavy-lidded and suspicious. His skinny frame looks lost in his sweat-stained white shirt and black pants in need of pressing. For a guy who just yesterday was hale and hearty enough to stack furniture in Nick's bookie joint, today he looks like a skeleton who's misplaced his skin. When he says, "Oh, hey there, Cantor," and opens the door, I get the picture; there's enough liquor on his breath to burn the place down if he lights a cigarette. He's still holding the bottle, a bottle of good Kentucky rye. He's also holding a gun. A .45 semi-auto that could put a hole in me the size of Brooklyn if I give him an excuse.

I breathe a bit easier when he drops the gun to his side as I walk in.

"Whiskey breakfast?" I say, and look around at the place. The living room's not as shabby as I expected in this tumbledown building. The furniture's not particularly classy, but it's not threadbare, either. It's all rather traditional, with an overstuffed couch and two club chairs in nubby maroon upholstery people were crazy about ten or fifteen years ago. The black-and-brown shag carpet is still in fairly good shape if in lousy taste, but the once-white walls are blotchy with cigarette-smoke stains. The window could use a good scrub-down. On the other hand, the grime on the window blurs the view to the not-so-pretty street.

The half decent if uninteresting furniture suggests that Mike can afford better than this crummy building. So what the hell is he doing here?

"Yeah, I've been drinking," he says, not quite slurring his words but not far from it. "See this gun? I've had it in my lap all night, my hand on the trigger. I've been drinking this whiskey and holding this gun because I'm scared, Cantor. Can you imagine that? A guy like me, a guy who used to work for the old waterfront mob when I was just a green kid and had to handle all kinds of nasty goings-on. You don't wanna know all the things I had to do. Some of it still keeps me lookin' over my shoulder.

Big Bill McGraw ran the docks back then. Ran it with guns and fists. He's dead now, y'know. Yeah, heart attack got him."

"So I've heard."

Mike gives that the kind of shrug that says, yeah, stuff like that happens, but so what. "Anyway," he says, going on with his story, "I saw a lotta killings, ugly, brutal killings. And I saw a lotta guys beaten to a pulp by Big Bill's thugs. But I survived, made it out alive and went to work for Nick. Best thing that ever happened to me. Sig Loreale arranged it when he sent Big Bill and his boys packing. I owe Loreale my life. What's wrong, Cantor? You look like I just told you your dog ran away. Here, have a drink." He holds the bottle out to me.

"I don't have a dog," I say. "And I'll pass on the whiskey. You have any coffee?" I do my best to keep my voice steady, which is tricky after my nerves jump at Mike's tidbit about Sig.

"Sorry, I finished the last of the coffee a coupla hours ago," he says.

I sit down in one of the club chairs, light a cigarette while Mike paces the carpet like a man trying to confuse his shadow.

I don't know Mike all that well, but I've seen him often enough at the bookie joint and here and there around town. He never came across as a guy who's scared of much. But here he is, a tough log of a guy, living in this crummy apartment, and afraid of every knock on the door. I need to know why. "Tell me something, Mike. Nick pay you well? You were his phone chief. You made sure the other phone guys got their betting slips right and handed in. Nick must've respected your smarts to give you that job."

"Sure, he paid me nice dough."

"Then why are you living in this—"

"Dump?" he says with a liquored-up laugh. "Sure it's a dump, but I got sentimental reasons for living here." His head's down now as he keeps walking the carpet, swaying a little with the bottle of rye in one hand, the .45 in the other. I don't know whether to feel sorry for the guy or be afraid of what's going on with that gun, so I'm tangled up with both.

He tries to talk again, a bit of spittle at the corner of his mouth. "I grew up in this place," he says. "And I like it. It's my neighborhood. I like the dockside people. They're my people. They survived the bloody days of Bill McGraw, just like me. And besides, it's nice being able to walk to work, not get my feet stepped on by some galoot on the subway. Nick's joint is only a few blocks from here, y'know. Oh yeah, sure. Of course you know."

"Uh-huh. Okay, live wherever you want," I say. "But listen, if Sig got you the job with Nick, what the hell are you afraid of? If Sig Loreale's on your side, I think you'd be pretty well protected."

Mike stops his pacing. He stands facing me, looking down at me in the chair. He's barely steady on his feet, the gun and the bottle of rye swaying in his hands. "You mean like Nick was protected? Lotta good Sig's protection did, huh."

I say nothing to that. There's nothing I can say. I give Mike a nod, a sad and angry nod.

"And who says Loreale's on my side?" Mike's laugh has no humor in it. Just terror barely blunted by a swig of rye. "I'm just another cog in his wheel of rackets, just like Nick was. And now Nick's dead. Maybe I'm next. Maybe everyone who worked for Nick will wind up dead. Maybe it's Loreale's way of firing people. No pink slip, no severance pay, just a bullet, or a stab in the back. Or a toss out a window." He flops down on the couch opposite me and puts the .45 back in his lap. "Or maybe my past is catching up with me."

It's a lousy business to watch someone fight for his life while he disintegrates into sawdust at the same time. There's still a spark in his eyes, while his body seems to crumble into the nubby fabric of the couch. But I can't let him disappear. He might yet dredge up a tidbit I can use, or a name I can trace that could help me find Nick's killer. "I don't blame you for being scared, Mike. Nick's death was too close to everyone's bone. But Sig didn't have any reason to kill Nick. And I can't see why he'd have any reason to kill you, or anyone else who worked in the bookie joint. So help me out here, Mike. Did Nick have any enemies you know about and I don't? Did you see anyone try to move in on him?"

He looks at me through drunken eyes, his eyelids fighting to stay open. And then his eyes suddenly brighten, the bit of life's spark flaring up, and a smile spreads slowly, uneasily, across his tired face. "Oh yeah," he says, "I forgot. You and Nick were longtime pals. Since you were kids, yeah? And now you think he held out on you about anyone who didn't like him? Why would he do that, Cantor?" He takes another swig from the bottle.

"No, Nick didn't hold out on me," I say. "But I didn't work in his bookie joint. I didn't see who came in, who was friendly and who wasn't. So maybe you saw someone who tried poking his finger in Nick's gut. Think, Mike. Did you ever see anyone who wasn't one-hundred percent? Someone who somehow made it past Freddie Holmes?" I'm hoping for a description, or better yet, the name of the punk who threatened Nick in his apartment. If I know the identity of the punk, I might get a line on who he worked for, who was crazy enough to make a move on Sig, who was nasty enough to kill Nick Fortunato and on whose orders.

I'm losing Mike to the whiskey again. "Past Freddie?" he mumbles, his chin on his chest. "Nothin' gets past Freddie. No way. Freddie's a…you know, he's a…Freddie's a sharp guy." He starts to lean sideways on the couch. The bottle of rye slips from his hand to the floor.

I'm up from the chair, stub out my smoke in an ashtray with one hand while my other hand shakes Mike by the chin. "Who are you afraid of, Mike? Who's a tough guy like you afraid of? Who do you think might've had it in for Nick?"

He rouses into a little more awareness, but not by much. "I

dunno," he says, his mouth barely working now. "Mebbe Abby knows somethin'. She's pals with Loreale, y'know."

Yeah, I know.

Chapter Eight

When Judson gave me Abby's address, my eyebrows went up so high so fast they threatened to fly off my head. I don't care how generous an employer Nick might've been; an office manager, even a right-hand to the boss, is never going to get the kind of salary it takes to pay the monthly rental on Central Park West.

The street is lined with some of the city's classiest buildings, most built in the 1920s and '30s when architects were either fooling around with fancy European-style goo-gaws all over the façades, or experimenting with the sleek sexiness of Art Deco. Some of the buildings even combine both, an audacious New York mishmash made gorgeous.

Abby's building is the Art Deco type, with warm yellow-gold stonework in triangular patterns at the entrance and a black, cream, and chrome-accented lobby just waiting for a Fred Astaire and Ginger Rogers dance number.

During the ride up the elevator to the twenty-first floor, I run through various scenarios that could provide Abby with the fistfuls of cash she needs to live here. Some make me laugh, some make me cringe. Some even scare me.

The twenty-first floor hallway is as sleek and dance-worthy as the lobby.

I find Abby's apartment halfway down the hall.

My morning improves a minute or so after I press the buzzer and Abby opens the door. Abby's a better sight in her doorway than Mike Landers was in his. She's a knockout in a silky black satin robe that goes all the way to her ankles, the hem tickling the feathery edge of her black satin backless slippers. Her dark hair, still a little tousled from bed, catches light from the hallway. She could pass for a movie star, the kind whose movies usually feature a good looking dame on the arm of the more suave variety of gangster.

Her eyes, usually calm with easy confidence, tighten at the sight of me. "You shouldn't be here, Cantor," she says, that deep-wine drawl of hers almost but not quite soothing the sting of essentially being told to get lost.

She starts to close the door in my face but I push it open. "But I *am* here," I say, "and I'm not leaving."

We stare at each other in the doorway. There's a tiny speck of defiance in her eyes' dark centers, a cold speck that chills me. I'm sure Abby sees the defiance in my eyes, too, but my defiance is different. It's not cold, it's not hot. I'm just a wall that won't budge.

She holds her own in our standoff until she eventually gets the message that I'm not going anywhere, and her expression reluctantly softens. She even manages a little smile. It's about as warm as a funeral announcement. "All right," she says, opening the door wider, "come in, though I don't know what good it will do you."

I walk past her and into the vestibule. "Mike Landers seems to think it might do me some good."

"Oh? How is Mike? He and Nick were good pals. Drinking buddies, or so I've heard. I guess he's taking Nick's death pretty hard. Or maybe he's worried I'll replace him as phone chief." She says all this with the chattiness of someone busy watering houseplants.

"How about a bit of both," I say. Somebody's got to stand up for Mike's broken heart, since it's clear the new boss lady isn't interested. "I guess you're still trying to do business with Sig?"

She obviously hears the not-so-subtle sarcasm in my voice, and doesn't like it. "And I suppose you still want to warn me off? Don't bother. I'm a big girl, Cantor. I can take care of myself."

"I don't doubt it," I say. "But will you take care of Mike and the other guys who worked for Nick, or are you going to give them the shove?"

She gives that a *tsk* with a toss of her head. "Of course not. Mike and the rest of Nick's crew are the best around. I'd be a fool to toss them over. I'll keep the shop closed for a while, let things cool down and give me time to make my plans, and then everyone will get back to business." She warms up a little. Her eyes brighten with the friendliness of someone who's just had an idea. "There's fresh coffee on. Care for some?"

That's the best offer I've had all morning. "Black, no sugar."

She looks over her shoulder as she walks out of the vestibule. "That's you, Cantor, all strength, no sweetness." She finishes it with a throaty little laugh.

I'm tempted to tell her that Lily Vardanian had a different opinion of me last night, but decide to keep that lovely memory to myself.

I follow Abby into the living room. Her slippers slap lightly against the soles of her feet as she walks. "Have a seat," she says, and wanders into the kitchen.

The living room decor is up-to-date high design, with clean lines but warm with blond wood furniture, colorful upholstery, and expensive taste. And I'll be damned, first-rate Abstract Expressionist paintings hang on the walls: a Rothko of blues and oranges that invites you to dive inside; a Lee Krasner in tight, wildly emotional swirls of black on white; and an Arshile Gorky of reds, yellow, blues, and blacks that induce feelings of marching to nowhere.

None of the paintings came from me. This is all big-league gallery stuff, the kind of art that gets top dollar forked over by the big museums or by rich collectors who think of themselves as hip and cool despite their nights out at the opera.

The top-of-the-line art and the high-style furniture tell me that not only does Abby have good taste, but a very deep pocketbook. Or somebody does.

There's a lot I don't know about Abby, and now I have the queasy feeling that there may be a lot I never knew about Nick.

I take my coat and cap off, toss them over the arm of a rust-colored chair, and make myself comfortable in the matching chair nearby. A coffee table, its high polish shining in the late morning sun through a window, separates me from a pale blue couch across the room. The blue-and-green plaid drapes are open, affording a view of the sky, Central Park, and the equally fancy if older-money Fifth Avenue apartment buildings on the other side of the park. I can almost feel the cash in my wallet wiggle in appreciation of the pricey view that comes with this pricey apartment.

Abby comes back into the living room with my cup of coffee and a cup for herself. After giving me mine, she sits across from me on the couch, her satin robe slithering along her body. The collar slides open a little at the top as she leans forward to put her cup on the coffee table. She doesn't move to cover herself up.

The slight mound of Abby's creamy skin through the open robe is distracting, and she knows it. It's why she's wearing a half-smile, a slight upturn at a corner of her mouth, a smile meant more for her enjoyment than mine.

Still smiling, she leans back into the couch. "Cantor," she says, "there's really nothing more I can tell you about Nick's death and my conversation with Sig, so let's—"

"Can't tell me or won't tell me?" I take a sip of coffee. It's strong, stronger than I expected, but after the initial kick it mellows out, as good coffee should, and helps keep me focused on why I'm here and not on that glimpse of flesh above Abby's robe.

"All right, I won't tell you," she says. "Look, maybe we don't know each other very well, but we've been acquaintances for a long time. I thought you understood that I really do like you, Cantor. I thought I made that clear when I was at your apartment last night. So please believe me when I tell you that the less you know, the better."

"You mean you know who killed Nick?"

"No, I don't know."

"But you might have an idea."

"Even I don't want to go there, Cantor."

I take another sip of coffee, using the moment to decide just how hard and how far to push, or maybe take another road altogether. "Then let's go somewhere else," I say. "Let's go to where you tell me how you afford all this expensive furniture and artwork and live at this very exclusive address."

"How I live is none of your business, Cantor." She says it as if I had the nerve to rummage around in her underwear drawer.

"It's my business if it's connected to Nick's death."

"Well, it isn't. How's the coffee?"

"Fine," I say, taking another sip. "But I suppose I wouldn't expect anything less from someone with your obvious good taste. You wouldn't have cheap anything, not even coffee. Now that we've gotten your sophisticated taste out of the way, let's get back to Nick's death, or don't you give a damn about the guy who trusted you to keep an eye on his business?"

"Of course I care, but life goes on."

"So you won't help me find Nick's killer?"

"I would if I could, but I—what's wrong, Cantor? Am I boring you?"

She's laughing softly when she says it. I guess she finds it funny that I'm having a hard time keeping my eyes open.

The coffee. She's drugged the coffee.

My head sways on my neck, but I manage to look up at Abby, who's become a smiling blur in a whirling room. Every muscle and bone in my body feels like they're dissolving, and then the world goes dark and silent as a tomb.

Chapter Nine

"That's it. Come on, come on," a voice drones in my ears as if through a long tunnel stuffed with cotton, while something seems to be pecking at my cheek. "Come on, Cantor," the droning voice says again, a little clearer now, but not much. I think the voice is familiar but I can't quite place it since it's still muffled inside the remnants of that tunnel of cotton.

The pecks at my cheek become less like pecks and more like pats. The pats get a little harder, and one is almost a slap. That's when my eyes snap open and I'm surprised to see Chickie D'Andrea's chubby face above mine, his slightly bulging eyes half hidden by the brim of his fedora pulled low. I'm surprised because Chickie's the kind of shlumpy guy you feel sorry for but you're never quite sure why, not the sort of guy who'd be involved in whatever the hell he's involved in after Abby drugged me. Part of it is the way he dresses, like the gray suit he's wearing now, an off-the-rack job I wouldn't be caught dead in. If I'm not careful, though, I might end up dead anyway, because under that suit jacket is the bulge of a gun. That's the trouble with cheap suits; the tailoring doesn't figure in gun-bulge.

"Hey, here you are," he says. He's got a voice smooth as a rolling fog. He's famous for it. Right now it's only slightly more comforting than his fleshy-lipped smile. "Welcome back."

I'm awake, more or less. My limbs feel spongy, but I manage to sit up, more or less. The first thing I see beyond Chickie is that Rothko painting, its misty blues and oranges scrambling my still fuzzy vision. But the Rothko lets me know that I'm still in Abby's apartment, still in the same chair where I drank the spiked coffee.

I'm slowly aware that Abby's walking into my field of vision and stands near Chickie. She's not in her black silk robe anymore. She's in a slender, dark green skirt and a white cotton blouse with puffy sleeves, the kind pirates wear. She has one hand on her hip while she looks me over as if she's apologizing to me and laughing at me at the same time.

"I'm sorry, Cantor," she says, reaching down to stroke my cheek. "But I was tired of arguing with you."

My lips feel like rubber tires. My tongue feels and tastes like that, too, so when I say, "So you drugged me?" the words are so mangled they're barely words at all.

"Well, I knew you'd balk if I told you I'd called Chickie while I was in the kitchen," she says. "I'd hoped you'd listen to him if you were too stubborn to listen to me. Spiking your coffee was the only thing I could think of to keep you here until Chickie arrived." She shrugs and smiles as if she finds the whole business a little funny. "No hard feelings?"

"Don't know yet," I say, still having trouble getting words over my tongue and past my lips. "What . . . what time is it? How long have I been here?"

"It's a little after one o'clock," she says. "You've been out less than an hour. How do you feel? Maybe coffee will help?" Adding, "Real coffee, this time, I promise," with what she thinks is a good-natured tweak of my chin.

It just makes me dizzy again.

Abby leaves for the kitchen to brew what I hope will be real honest-to-god coffee.

I'm alone with Chickie. He pulls the other chair over to face me, opens his suit jacket, sits down and pushes his fedora back on his head. A tuft of his mousy-brown crew cut pokes out from under his hat and looks silly above his chubby face.

There's nothing silly about the butt of his revolver poking out from his shoulder rig.

Seeing Chickie's gun reminds me to check if my own gun is still in its rig. It is. I guess Chickie isn't planning to kill me today. Either that or he's a negligent tough guy.

My lips are starting to feel more like flesh and less like old rubber. Words come out of my mouth a little easier. "So you're in on whatever deal Abby's got cooking?"

"Whatever Abby's got cooking is her own business," he says and leans forward, arms on his knees, in an attitude of buddy-to-buddy. It's not that I don't like Chickie. I've never had a problem with him. It's just hard to buddy up to someone I feel sorry for for no particular reason, and Chickie's clumsy pal act isn't making it any easier. Neither is his grin, or his gun. "I'm here to help you, Cantor," he says.

"If talking to me with a gun under your arm is your idea of help, Chickie, you'll excuse me if I'd rather work alone."

He gives that a friendly snicker. "Look," he says, "I'm an odds guy. You know that. I'm the guy Nick relied on to make sure the odds coming in on the wires were kosher, know what I mean? Nick knew I could spot finagled odds a mile away, crooked odds that low-rent chiselers think they can get away with. I know good odds and lousy odds when I see 'em, even if they're on the up-and-up. And from what I hear, you're up against lousy odds."

"It wouldn't be the first time," I say. "People have been wanting me to fail, disappear, or drop dead since the first time I put on a suit. But you're not going to talk me out of walking away from this, Chickie. Abby couldn't, and you can't either. I'm going to find out who killed Nick. Somebody has to, even if you and Abby and Sig and the cops don't give a damn who killed him."

He sits up again, his round, slightly bulgy eyes open wide with the pained expression of a kid nobody wants to play with in the schoolyard. "Now wait a minute, Cantor. I happen to care about what happened to Nick."

"Yeah? Then how come you came running when Loreale's newest sidekick beckoned?" I nod toward the kitchen, where we hear the rattle of Abby taking cups and saucers from a cabinet.

Chickie leans back in his chair, more annoyed now than insulted. "Don't believe everything you see, Cantor. Listen, I know you and Nick went way back. Everyone knows it. But when it came to his bookie operation, you were just another customer. You weren't on the inside of the operation. I was. I had Nick's trust in ways you couldn't. That trust meant plenty to me. And now some sonuvabitch snuffed out a guy who treated me with respect, who appreciated my talents. You don't find guys like that too often. You know what I'm talking about, Cantor. So yeah, I give a damn about what happened to Nick. And when I say I want to help you find out about it, I mean it. Better you than the cops, if you know what I mean."

"I wouldn't worry about the cops, Chickie," I say. "Sig controls the cops. You know that. If Sig wants the cops out, they're out, which is just as well. They'd only get in my way."

Chickie nods at that, laughs a little. "Don't they always?" he says. "But you've got to believe me. I'm here to help you find Nick's killer."

"You've told Abby that?"

"Not yet. I will when, y'know, when the time's right."

"Uh-huh. I hope your watch doesn't run slow."

His eyes grow a bit rounder, protrude a bit more under his lids. His fleshy lips purse. I wouldn't say he looks like he's about to cry, maybe just whimper a little. "Why do I get the feeling you don't trust me, Cantor?"

Abby comes in with the coffee before I can tell Chickie all my reasons why trusting him right now is an iffy proposition, starting with the gun he made sure I saw.

Abby puts the tray with the cups, saucers, and coffeepot on the table, pours everyone a cup, and hands them around. I bring my cup to my lips, but hesitate to drink until Abby and Chickie drink theirs first. Neither of them falls into a faint. I guess I can trust the coffee.

It's certainly strong, strong enough to clear the last of the cotton from my head.

Abby takes her coffee to the couch, sits down in that provocative way she has, each section of her body sinuously carving the air around her. It's all look-but-don't-touch, though. The bets are still open about just who Abby allows a touch. "Well, Cantor?" she says, "has Chickie talked sense into you? I assume that after seeing me at Sig's you have reason not to trust me. But I'd hoped you'd listen to Chickie."

"And I guess both of you just have only the best intentions regarding my safety."

"Why wouldn't we?" Abby says.

"Well, that's the question of the hour, isn't it." I reach inside my suit jacket.

Chickie's .38 comes out fast.

So much for trust.

I say, "Do you always pull a gun on someone taking out a pack of smokes?"

He slips the gun back into his rig, though he doesn't seem to want to, but does it anyway. "Now listen, Cantor," he says, "can't blame a guy for being careful around you. You have a reputation for—"

"For what? Doing what I have to do to survive?"

"Well, yeah, something like that."

I light my smoke, take a deep drag, let it out slowly while I take in the sights: Abby on the couch, sipping her coffee, her eyes on me like a jungle cat; Chickie sitting opposite me, swallowing a gulp of coffee and avoiding looking at me at all. What an odd pair they make.

Too odd. One of them wants me out of her way; the other one offered to help me then changed his mind and decided maybe he wants to kill me.

And neither of them are leading me closer to the mystery of what happened to Nick.

Not yet.

"Well," I say, taking a last sip of coffee before I get up from the chair, "thanks for the coffee and the nap. I'm sure you two have things you want to discuss, so I'll be seeing you."

Chickie just gives me a quick look and a nod as I head to the door. I hear Abby purring, "Goodbye, Cantor."

You'd never guess that behind a steel slab where a doorway should be on a nondescript little corner building on Twelfth Avenue under the West Side Highway, across from the midtown West Side docks, is an office with a room-size basement vault holding paintings, sculptures, and other treasures waiting for delivery. They'll stay there as long as the clients who hired me to risk my life to steal them pay up. Most do.

You can't enter the office from the street. The only entrance is through the alleys behind the scruffy mom-and-pop shops, greasy spoon luncheonettes, down-at-the-heel saloons, and piece-goods factories in small, sagging brick buildings that line the block. But despite the soot, the heavy smells from the food joints, the sharp stink of stale beer, despite the trash overflowing the curbside wire baskets, the discarded newspapers flying around the sidewalk and in the gutter, despite all that, the neighborhood is made homey by its comforting medley of sounds. It's a New York music of the human chatter in the street, the whoosh of traffic overhead on the elevated highway, the moody bellow of ship's horns and lonely clang of buoy bells on the Hudson River. This dockside symphony trails me, soothes me, as I walk through the alleys to the back door of my office.

This door's a steel slab, too, but my key unlocks it, lets me slide it open. Judson has the only other key to the place.

Inside, Judson's at his desk checking through a ledger, no doubt balancing everything in our stash of purloined goods against anyone who needs to pay up. He's a whiz at such things. He's a whiz at most things that need brainwork. If IBM knew about Judson, they wouldn't bother developing those newfangled electronic brains. From what I've seen in the papers and on the TV news, those machines take up whole rooms. Judson takes up a lot less space. All he needs is a desk, a chair, a pencil, paper, and a telephone, and the next thing you know he's privy to whatever information the power players or the Law tries to hide.

Fashion-wise, he's graduated from the tee-shirts and jeans he wore when I first fished him off the streets. These days he favors dark chinos and snappy cardigans over white shirts buttoned to the neck. He still hasn't made friends with ties. And he hasn't given up his black leather motorcycle jacket. It's hanging on the rack behind his desk.

Today's cardigan is a red, tan, and brown argyle number. Works well with Judson's brown hair and his gold wire-rimmed specs. If it wasn't for that black leather jacket behind him, you'd swear he's a regular college Joe, the kind that gets PhDs in ancient languages or complicated math. But Judson wouldn't need a classroom to learn the languages or figure the math. He could do that on his own if he was of a mind to. College life would only bore him. Ferreting out the secrets of cooing co-eds or the petty power squabbles among the faculty wouldn't hold the same tang for Judson as uncovering where a gangster hid his cash, his girlfriend, or a body, or developing a network of people or places where one can get certain services, no questions asked. Judson's my encyclopedia, my telephone book, my trowel.

He hands me a couple of messages when I park myself on

the edge of his desk: one's from a client up in the tonier parts of Westchester who's in the market for a Renaissance Madonna and could I get it from the Church of the Holy Something-Or-Other in Rome, he's forgotten the name. This guy's a pain in the ass. Big desires, shallow pockets. "Call him back," I tell Judson. "Tell him I'll look into it, but don't tell him when."

The other message is from a curator of decorative arts at a small museum upstate. I've worked with this guy before. He's good for quick cash. I'll call him myself another time. I still have stuff to deal with today, like making sure Nick gets a decent funeral, one with a fancy casket, lots of flowers, and all the other trimmings.

Judson says, "How did those addresses I gave you work out?" as I walk to the door of my private office.

"So far, so good," I say, and walk inside.

I close the door behind me, take off my coat and cap, hang them on the rack, and fold myself down limp as an old pleated curtain into my desk chair. I'm still feeling the lingering effect of the knockout drops Abby put in my coffee.

It's a big chair behind a big desk. The chair and desk are part of the top-of-the-line furnishings I've outfitted the place with. Since I risk my life for the money I make, I figure I've earned my console TV cabinet, my expensive oxblood leather couch, my pale green club chair whose upholstery is as soft and welcoming as Lily's arms were last night.

I have to see Lily again. I have to experience her again.

All the fancy furnishings, the closet full of changes of clothes, the shower stall, the refrigerator stocked with food, and of course a supply of Chivas scotch, make my office not just a workplace, but a comfortable place to lay low when cops or others with bad intentions get too close to whatever I'm up to. Only a handful of people know about this place. Even the ownership title doesn't have my name. Thanks to my excellent lawyer, you'd have to dig through enough paperwork that felled whole forests and still probably never find my name.

I pull out the Yellow Pages from a desk drawer, find a listing for a funeral parlor near Nick's apartment, Esposito's on Sixth Avenue. Sounds about right. Nick was Italian. He wasn't especially religious, a lapsed Catholic as they say, but I bet he'd like to know he'll spend eternity among his people.

A receptionist answers the phone. She has a sweet voice but with a tone of solemnity that could only be the voice of someone who prefers a wardrobe of severely cut black suits. I ask if Esposito's can arrange a full funeral quickly. She tells me to hold on, she'll connect me with Mr. Esposito.

A few seconds later, a male voice comes on the line. "This is John Esposito. How may I help you?"

I give him the same question I gave to the receptionist.

"Certainly," he says. "And what was the loved one's name?"

If Nick wasn't already dead he would die laughing if he'd heard himself referred to as my loved one. Well, I guess he was, in his way. I really did love the guy. "Nick—uh, let's go with his full name on the headstone. Nicholas Anthony Fortunato. He passed away last night."

"Oh!" Esposito cracks in my ear. "It seems Mr. Fortunato's remains have already been taken care of."

"Taken care of? What do you mean, taken care of? Someone already arranged for his funeral?" Two possibilities pop up: Abby or Sig, or maybe they arranged it together. Maybe it was their way of atoning for picking Nick's business apart before his body was even cold.

"Taken care of, yes, in a way," Esposito says.

"Well, when's the funeral, and where?"

"I'm sorry, I'm afraid I wasn't clear. Mr. Fortunato's remains were cremated late last night. Well, three o'clock in the morning, actually."

Sig. Only Sig has the clout to have Nick's body released from the medical examiner's office fast and cremated even faster. Only

Sig could arrange for all trace of Nick disappear. The sickening question rolling around in my head is: why does he want to?

I press the now nervously breathing undertaker a little more. "All right, then, Mr. Esposito, where were the ashes delivered?"

"They weren't. A—uhm, a gentleman," he says as if gagging on the term—"came here and picked up the urn."

"And the gentleman's name?"

"He said his name is Mr. Smith."

"Uh huh. I bet he did. And I suppose he gave you a wad of bills with pictures of dead presidents. Okay, we'll skip that bit of an illegal transaction. What did Mr. Smith look like?"

I can hear Esposito's throat close up in a tight swallow, followed by a short, sharp breath. "He, well, he was a big gentleman. Bulky."

And I bet his friends and enemies know him as Bensonhurst Benny.

Chapter Ten

My first words to Sig after he answers the phone pour out in a disgusted gush: "Don't you have any respect for anyone, alive or dead, Sig?"

"I beg your pardon, Cantor?" he says in that ponderous way he has that crushes every bone in my spine. "What are you talking about?

"I'm talking about a guy you've known since he was a kid, a guy who was your partner in the bookie business, who built up that business with smarts and hard work. That's who I'm talking about. A guy who made bagfuls of cash for you, money you really didn't need, Sig. You've got enough money to buy whole countries. Nick paid you every dime anyway because he—"

"I should remind you that it was Miss O'Neill who figured up my dividend."

Dividend. Hah. What a slick term for a cut of the action. "On Nick's instructions, Sig. On Nick's instructions. But never mind that. I just got off the phone with that undertaker, Esposito. You had Nick cremated, didn't you, Sig. You didn't even think enough of the guy to give him a decent funeral where his friends and the people who worked for him could say their goodbyes, and where Nick could be buried with his own kind. What did you do, Sig? Pay off the medical examiner to release the body in the middle of the night? Threaten him? Y'know what? Never mind that, either. Just give me the urn with his ashes. I'll keep it at my place so that the last of Nick Fortunato can at least be with someone who gave a damn about him."

"Your sense of honor is misplaced, Cantor, and so is your request for Mr. Fortunato's ashes. You see, I do not have them."

"Oh?" I practically bark it. "Then who does? Where did Benny take them? Yeah, I know it was Benny you sent to pick them up. Even Esposito had a hard time calling Bensonhurst Benny a gentleman."

"No one has them, Cantor," Sig says, annoyed now with the conversation. "Except, perhaps, the bellies of the less discerning fish in the East River."

My hand grips the phone so hard my knuckles hurt. My jaw's clamped shut so tight I can't get any words past my teeth, can't spit the curses I want to land in Sig's ears.

The only voice that's still able to come through the phone is Sig's. "I warned you, Cantor, to stay out of this situation."

I have to force myself to speak, to get words out. They come out as a near whisper. "And now you're going to have to tell me why, Sig. And while you're at it, tell me what's Abby O'Neill's involvement? And Chickie D'Andrea's? I'm not buying that song and dance that it's simply a business arrangement for Abby to assume control of Nick's bookie joint. I stopped believing that fairytale after she drugged me, and Chickie pulled a gun on me."

"You always did lead a dangerous life," Sig says, "no matter how hard I tried to protect you. Goodbye, Cantor." He hangs up, the click of the phone as frosty as turning his back.

There are places I go when I need solace or stimulus or just to get a bit of warm and cozy. The Green Door Club is one of them, where I go when I need a little romance among my kind. My office is another, where I can bask in the rewards of sticking my finger in the Law's eye. And when I'm hungry, when I need good, basic New York food, the best coffee in town, and the ask-no-questions accept-all-types company of the denizens of my theater district neighborhood, I come here to Pete's Luncheonette, a no-frills joint down the street from my apartment. The black-and-green checkerboard linoleum floor, the marble-top counter and tables, have all been here since the place opened sometime during the Coolidge administration. It's got the welcoming aromas of freshly brewed coffee and heavy wool winter coats hanging on the coatrack or on the backs of chairs. It's got customers who either pay me no mind or just give me a nod before going back to scanning the casting notices in the show-biz dailies, or figuring the odds in the racing forms, or catching the latest hoochie-koochie photos in the *New York Daily Mirror*, a newspaper of no journalistic distinction but plenty of lively photos and snappy writing. Best of all, Pete's Luncheonette has Doris, the thin-faced, pink-uniformed waitress who's been here almost as long as the linoleum. There's enough street-savvy in her eyes to fill a police blotter. I've known Doris since her hair was brown and permanent-waved. Her hair's almost all gray now, and pulled back in a knot under her waitress's cap. A pencil is always lodged behind her ear.

She gives me a welcoming smile, the warmth behind it one of the reasons I stay a regular customer. That and the terrific coffee, a java more trustworthy than the spiked brew Abby slipped me. "You look hungry," Doris says, and pours me a hot mug as I slide onto a stool at the counter.

"I'm plenty hungry," I say. "I never got breakfast, and now it's almost two-thirty, way past my lunch. Give me a pastrami on rye, heavy on the pastrami, light on the mustard."

Doris gives my order to the kitchen on her way down the counter to serve another customer, a veteran actress neighbor of mine just back from a hinterlands touring company of one of last year's Broadway hits. It's been a while, I suspect, since she's played the big time, if she ever did. But she earns a living in a tough racket, so good for her. We give each other a neighborly wave as I go to a phone booth in the back.

I drop my dime into the slot, dial Lily's hotel, ask the clerk to connect me to her room, and close the phone booth door. I like my neighbors well enough but this won't be a conversation I want to share with them. Let 'em get their own love life.

I want to see Lily tonight. I want her arms around me again. I want my hands on her.

Her room phone rings. It rings several times. She doesn't answer.

I hang up, breathe out my disappointment, and remind myself that she's here on a job. Stupid of me to think she'd hang around in her hotel room all day.

Doris comes back with my pastrami sandwich as I slide again onto my stool at the counter. "Now you look *sad* and hungry," she says. "I've seen that hangdog look on your face before, usually when some cutie pie has eyes for someone other than you. Y'know, Cantor, under those scars on your face, you're not bad lookin'."

I give her a smile, slide my fingers under her chin. "My dear darlin' Doris, you sure know how to lift the spirits. Ever think of switching sides of the street?"

"Save it!" she says with a good-humored laugh. "I'm too old for you, and anyway I've got a husband I spent thirty years training. But I'm serious about those scars, Cantor. Ever consider plastic surgery? I hear they do wonders these days. Even a lot of the movie stars go under the knife, y'know."

"My scars tell the story of my life," I say. "Each one is a souvenir of my survival."

"You lead a tough life, Cantor. I hope the rewards are worth it."

I think about last night, about Lily's body against mine. I think about the heat of her, the sweat we shared, the tingle in my loins I still carry with me.

Through a smile that's as tender as it is smutty, I say, "Oh, the rewards are worth it, Doris. They are definitely worth it."

"Then why do you look like you just lost your best friend?"

She could have said anything else. She could have said I look like I'd been mugged, or thrown down the stairs, or that my apartment was ransacked and my car wrecked, but when Doris said I look like I just lost my best friend, she nailed me to the wall. I don't know if Nick was my best friend, I don't know if I've ever had a best friend, but Nick Fortunato was in my life long enough to qualify. That's gotta count for something.

I take a sip of coffee, let it start my heart beating again. And when I'm sure I'm alive, I say, "Doris, you ever play the horses?"

"Now and then. Why? Is that why you look down in the dumps? Did you lose a bundle?"

The pastrami sandwich fills my belly. The coffee kicks me into gear. "Nope. You got it right the first time, Doris." I toss two bucks on the counter as I get up: a buck for the sandwich and coffee and a buck for Doris.

But Doris, street-savvy Doris, reaches across the counter and grabs my arm before I can walk away. "You always were a big tipper, Cantor. It's one of the reasons I like you, among your other charming if rough qualities. But you're lousy at hiding your hurts. They're all over you like a rain-soaked shirt. Whoever it is you lost, do me a favor and don't get yourself killed over it. I'd miss these big tips of yours."

I take her hand from my arm, lightly kiss her fingers like they do in the movies. "Or I could just put you in my will," I say with the only smile that's felt good all day.

Chapter Eleven

Harlem's main drag, 125th Street, is bustling this afternoon with shoppers and other folks going about their business. It's a scene not much different than any other shopping street all over the city, except that the shoppers and everyone else here are Negroes. I stick out like a sore white thumb.

A nearby school must've let out a few minutes ago because a bunch of little girls holding schoolbags skip along the sidewalk in a giggling knot. Some of the girls are as young as six or seven, some verging on teenage years. They look up at me and gawk before they resume their giggling.

No doubt I'm a sight to see, the only white person on Harlem's central stem, and a white dame in a gentleman's duds and cap to boot. One little girl, an adorable kid of maybe twelve, with curiosity in her eyes and a blue bow in her hair, turns back to look at me. I give her a wave. She gives me a smile but then turns away fast, the way little girls do when shyness overwhelms fascination.

Thirty years ago or so, during the hot-cha days of the Roaring Twenties and into the Thirties, my shy little friend and her pals might not have been surprised by my presence in her neighborhood. Back in those days, white folks would come uptown for a night at Harlem's world-famous nightspots, places like the Savoy Ballroom, where Chick Webb's swing band whipped up the Lindy-hopping crowds, or Small's Paradise, known for its singing waiters and 6 a.m. shows, and most famous of all, The Cotton Club, where Duke Ellington provided elegant music for top shelf shows and high line talent. The Cotton Club was so exclusive it allowed in only white patrons, and shady enough to be owned by one of the town's major mobsters, Owney Madden.

Another reason my little friend might not have been so surprised by my presence in those days was Harlem's tolerance at the time for people like me: women in suits, men in gowns, dancing in the clubs, singing in the nightspots, carousing at parties not for the sexually faint-of-heart.

These days, all of that's gone, well, most of it anyway. Despite the jazz scene moving down to Fifty-second Street, where the more elite or timid whites feel more comfortable, Harlem still has its soul. I hear it in the tunes coming out of radios in passing cars, or through the doors of record shops and cocktail lounges. The music's called Rhythm and Blues these days, and without it, pretty white boy rock-'n'-roller and teenage heartthrob Elvis Presley wouldn't have a note to sing.

When I go around the corner onto a residential stretch of 126th Street, things are quieter, with only a few pedestrians on the street. A group of middle-aged guys, some in WW2 army veterans' garrison caps, some in fedoras or thin-brimmed trilbys, are hanging around a stoop of one of the brownstone row-houses, schmoozing away the afternoon. A few give me a side-eye as I walk by, some give me a sarcastic smile. One guy even spits on the sidewalk in front of me.

I say, "Afternoon, gentlemen," tip my cap, and just keep walking. Their hostility is nothing I haven't dealt with before. Doesn't matter what neighborhood I'm in, or the skin color, accent, or religion of the residents, my just being alive in my own way breaks a lot of people's rules.

I find the address Judson gave me, walk up the front stairs, and press the buzzer for "Holmes."

A few seconds later, I hear Freddie's voice over the intercom. "Who is it?"

"It's me, Freddie. Cantor Gold."

He buzzes me in.

The hallway's one of those nineteenth-century jobs of well-oiled woodwork and thick floral carpeting, though the dark green brocade wallpaper is bubbling here and there, ready to peel.

Freddie's place is on the third floor. The carpeted stairs muffle my footsteps, but not the sounds of life coming from inside various apartments: a radio playing a smooth R & B tune, a baby crying, a woman laughing.

Freddie's in his open doorway when I arrive on the third-floor landing.

His suspenders are down at his sides, his white shirt open at the neck, a man comfortably at home in his rental castle. "I figured you'd show up sooner or later," he says, cocking his head to usher me in.

Inside, the place is cozily furnished, with well-kept old-fashioned, heavily upholstered furniture and freshly vacuumed flowery rugs.

"How 'bout a drink?" he says. "Or maybe some coffee? The wife's got a pot brewin' in the kitchen."

It's just now hitting three-thirty, not too early for a little alcohol pick-me-up. "I'll take a scotch," I say, taking my cap off. "Chivas if you got it."

"I got it," he says on his way to a cabinet against a wall. He pulls a couple of glasses and a bottle from a well-stocked supply, pours us both a drink, and hands me mine. Lifting his glass, he says, "Here's to Mr. Nick Fortunato, a sweet guy who's got no business bein' dead."

After we both swallow, he wipes his mouth with the back of his hand, gives me that size-'em-up look he's famous for, and says, "You really think you're gonna find whoever did it? That's why you're here, ain't it? See if I got any ideas about who might've done the killin'?"

"Well, do you?" I say. I open my coat and sit down in one of the big upholstered chairs. Freddie sits in another chair just like it across from me. Sunlight through a window behind him turns his gray hair a regal silver. It suits him. "No one can spot a wrong type better than you, Freddie. Ever see anyone around Nick you thought wasn't kosher?"

He takes his time answering, turning his whiskey glass in hand until finally he shrugs, his mind settling whatever it was he had to settle. "Sure I did. I saw plenty of sketchy types," he says. "But they'd be mostly small fry. Cheap money makin' wrong bets, if y'know what I mean. None of 'em got the bones to be killers."

"So you're not afraid of any of them? Or anyone else?"

He takes another swallow of his drink, leans back in his chair, his body at ease, his eyes, though, darkening over something inside him that isn't at ease at all. "I don't own no business. I don't own anything anyone would want to take from me. Not anymore. So I got no reason to think anyone would want to come after me and kill me—at least, no one in the bookie business." He downs the rest of his drink, purses his lips and furrows his brow in something deeper and sadder than mere anger.

Quietly, taking care not to stomp on whatever hurt Freddie's feeling, I say, "Mike Landers is scared out of his wits. He sat up all night with a gun in his lap and a whiskey bottle in his mouth, scared that whoever came after Nick might come after him, too. Any idea why he'd feel that way?"

My question seems to pull Freddie out of whatever misery he'd been mulling. He even laughs a bit, a sarcastic chuckle I wouldn't have expected from him, a guy with a reputation for loyalty. "Mr. Mike would like everybody to believe he's a tough guy from the docks. And maybe he used to be. But I been gettin' the feelin' lately that he's scared of his own shadow. Couldn't tell you why, though, 'cept I guess somethin' must've shook him. Miss Abby had to get on his back now and then about keepin' his mind focused on the telephone action."

That tidbit might turn out to be a bombshell, or it just might be an old man's gossip. I take another swallow of my drink, let it steady me, so that my tongue won't trip over my too-eager curiosity. "You saying Mike's afraid of Abby?"

A female voice answers as its owner walks into the living room. "Sure he is. And with good reason, too. How've you been, Cantor? Still a slick dresser, I see." It's Freddie's wife, Ida, wiping her hands on the plaid apron over her green cotton housedress. It's been a while since I've seen her. She's still a thin woman, always has been, but nicely heavy in the upstairs terrace, if sagging a bit now with age. Her hair, more salt-and-pepper gray than her husband's, is pulled back in a bun, the style drawing my attention to the soft remnants of her once girlishly pretty face. Her smile's warm and welcoming above her don't-miss-a-trick brown eyes. "Stand up and take off that coat," she says with a wave in my direction, "and let me see the rest of those threads."

I do as she says. "Good to see you, Ida. It's been a while. You haven't been down to the bookie joint much lately."

"Found better things to do with my time than take the coats and hats of folks too stupid to stop losing their money. I got me a job evenings in the back room of the Tuxedo Club over on Saint Nicholas Avenue. Easy work, good pay, and I get to sit down."

Meaning Ida's one of the crew of women who water down the bottles of booze.

She looks me over as she sits down on the arm of Freddie's chair. "You still carry those threads real nice, Cantor," she says. Her husband gives her a pat on her knee, which she likes. "So, either one of you cavaliers going to pour a lady a drink?" she says.

I'm still standing so I go over to the liquor supply, pull a glass, and say over my shoulder, "What'll you have, Ida?"

"Whatever you're having."

I pour her a Chivas, hand it to her, and sit back down again in my chair. "Listen, Ida, what did you mean that Mike Landers has good reason to be afraid of Abby?"

She takes a ladylike swallow of scotch, then says, "She's got too much ambition, that woman."

"Don't you think a woman can have ambition?"

"Sure, she can. But not the kind of ambition that knifes people in the back. Women like that are dangerous. Believe me, I know."

"Who'd Abby knife in the back, Ida?"

"Hah! Who didn't she? She even tried to get my Freddie fired, but Mr. Nick had more sense."

Freddie pats his wife's knee again, but a little less lovingly this time. "Now, Ida, don't go tellin' tales outta school."

I finish off the rest of my drink, try to square what Ida's telling me with what Abby said about keeping all of Nick's crew on the payroll. But I can't square it.

"Freddie," I say, "is that right? Did Abby try to fire you? Why?"

Even after enjoying the good scotch and sitting in his big, well upholstered chair, Freddie looks about as comfortable now as a man sitting on tacks. "Some things are best left be, Cantor. Makin' trouble ain't gonna fix what's past."

"Isn't finding Nick's killer worth making trouble?" I say.

"Not if—"

But Ida cuts him off. "Let Cantor do what she's gotta do, Freddie. Mr. Nick meant a lot to her for a long time from what I hear, and you just don't throw away that kind of loyalty like it was milk gone sour. So if knowing the truth about that Abby woman helps Cantor find who killed Mr. Nick, then you gotta tell her. Go on, tell her, 'cause if you don't tell her, I will."

"It ain't your story to tell, wife."

Ida gives him a sharp, annoyed poke to the shoulder. "Now you listen to me, Freddie Holmes. It's my story, too. And you know why. So I have just as much right to tell it as—"

"All right!" Freddie barks it like a pup in pain. "All right, I'll tell it." He looks up at his wife, then looks at me with that same purse-lipped, furrowed-brow look on his face I saw earlier, an expression about something within him more painful than mere sadness or anger. "It seems," he finally says, his voice tense and guttural, "that Miss Abby thought I was bad for business."

"You? Bad for the bookie business?" The idea is so ridiculous I can't believe a sharp cookie like Abby O'Neill would even bother to entertain it, except that Freddie Holmes isn't known to be a liar. "Everyone knows you're the best spotter in town," I say.

"Well, it wasn't my ability to spot bad trade that got in her way," he says. "It was my black skin. She thought a Black man shouldn't be workin' the door. She said it brought in the wrong type of clientele. And she had other plans for the joint." He says it with a sneer, the sneer of an old man who's seen a lot to sneer at in his life. "But Mr. Nick cut her off. He reminded her that he was the boss and that he does all the hirin' and firin' and that as far as he was concerned I could work the door as long as I could stand up."

I'm thrown back into something Abby said to me: that there's a lot about her I don't know. Damn right.

And something else I don't know. "Freddie, did Abby tell Nick what those other plans were?"

"He said nothin' to me about it."

There's a knot in my stomach getting tighter and bigger by the minute. I wonder if it popped out of my belly if it would have Sig Loreale's name all over it.

I get up from the chair, put my coat and cap back on. "Ida, always a pleasure. And Freddie, thanks for the drink and the information. I'll be seeing you."

On my way to the door, I hear Ida say, "You be careful, Cantor Gold." And then I hear what sounds like Freddie sobbing a little, and Ida comforting him. A husband and wife staying alive by love.

I should be so lucky.

I step inside the phone booth on the corner, dial Lily's hotel, tell the clerk to connect me to her room. My need to see her tonight, to have her arms around me, my mouth taste her, my hands explore her, has grown stronger since I heard Ida's whispers of comfort to Freddie's battered heart. I want that kind of warmth. I need it to melt the icy cold of Nick's death, Sig's threats, and the hatred choking Freddie's life.

There's no answer.

Chapter Twelve

The long drive from Harlem down to the Lower East Side gives me time to quiet my craving for Lily and my hurt for Freddie. Only my grief and anger over Nick's murder remain, the churning engine that's sent me here.

I find a parking spot along Second Avenue, just a few doors down from the brownstone I've come to visit, and the old woman who's lived there over fifty years. She's one of the last holdouts of the old crowd in a neighborhood changing from pushcart peddlers, piece-goods workers, and lovers of kosher pickles and pastrami on rye, to bodegas selling zesty Puerto Rican specialties, and soul food joints with the mouth-watering aroma of smoked ribs wafting into the street. This new population is joined by a recent trickle of writers, artists, and musicians priced out of Greenwich Village west of here, a bohemian bunch taken to calling this end of the neighborhood the East Village. Cute.

I'm here because the woman who lives in that brownstone, Esther "Mom" Sheinbaum, the most successful fence for stolen goods in the city's history, knows who's who and what's what among the grifters on the streets, the politicians in City Hall, the finance finaglers on Wall Street, and the Old Money lords of Fifth and Park Avenues. They've all done business with her, they all owe her. There isn't a secret she doesn't know or can't get about people who'd either pay or kill to keep their secrets from leaking. There's only one person whose secrets Mom doesn't know: Sig Loreale. Nobody will ever know Sig's secrets.

It just might be possible, though, that maybe Mom's caught a snippet here and there. She's certainly known Sig long enough. For that matter, so have I. And also for that matter, I've known Mom about as long as I've known Sig. While Sig was keeping an eye on me—and Nick—back in Coney Island, Mom was teaching me the difference between high line loot and cheap goods not worth my kiddie-thief's time.

So yeah, we've come a long way, Mom, Sig, and I, a long road paved with money, survival, and occasional moments of shaky trust.

At the top of the front stairs, while I wait for Mom to answer the doorbell, out of habit I straighten my tie, make sure the lapels of my overcoat are smooth, and my cap on straight.

She's not called Mom for nothing.

The door opens. Mom's formidable bulk stands in the doorway in an eye-straining paisley dress. In the late afternoon sunlight from the street, her silvery hair, styled in a modified bouffant hair-sprayed to stiffness, shimmers like an empress's crown. Seems appropriate, since her other nickname among the underworld's old-timers is the Empress of Crime. Her eyes, small and dark, don't appear to be happy to see me.

"This isn't a good time, Cantor," she says in the old Lower East Side sing-song and Old World accent that renders my name as *Kentuh*.

Mom may not always warm up to me, but she's never kept me out of her house. "It's important," I say.

"So important that you don't call first? What's the matter? You never heard of a telephone?"

"What's going on, Mom? Why the brush-off?"

"This is not a good time, I told you."

She starts to close the door. I push against it to stop it from closing, but Mom doesn't budge. She's a monument to stubbornness. "And I told *you* it's important," I say. "I need information, information you have or can get. I need the goods on some people." Stubborn or not, the old woman's no match for my determination. I slide past her and into the vestibule.

She doesn't try to stop me, because she can't. She makes her displeasure known with a hard, sharp *tsk*.

The aroma of honey cake floats through the house. There's always the aroma of honey cake in Mom's house, only this time the aroma is accompanied by voices drifting from the dining room, across the parlor and into the vestibule.

Everything inside me—my breath, the blood in my veins— threatens to come to a stop.

The look I give Mom, and the half-smile that comes with it, is part surprise, part curiosity, and part dread, the kind of dread that comes from suddenly knowing something you don't want to know. "Interesting company you keep," I say.

"So what," Mom says. "So you heard. Didn't I warn you? Didn't I say it wasn't a good time for you to show up? If your feelings got hurt, it's no fault of mine."

It's my turn to *tsk*. "It never is," I say with all the sincerity the lie deserves.

"Go ahead, make jokes," she says, waving a pudgy, be-ringed hand at me. "Jokes won't help you see which side of your bread's got the butter. Listen, *mommeleh*, why would you think I'd want to hurt you? I've known you since you were a kid, a little *pisher* with a satchel stuffed with stolen junk."

I don't bother reminding her that she once told me that the way I dress and my romantic preference for women disgusts her. I don't bother because it doesn't matter. Sure, it stung me pretty bad at the time but I got over it, at least enough to still do business with her. Mom's business brings me good money, and money is my armor against life's slings and poison arrows.

Money is my last laugh against all those very nice people who think my life is a sin, and the not-so-nice people, like cops, who hate the idea that I can afford a good lawyer.

I walk through the parlor, an old-fashioned room of heavy, overstuffed furniture of the type that was popular when the century was still young, and so were Mom and her now deceased husband when they bought the place. As I near the dining room, the sweet aroma of honey cake grows stronger, the voices in the room grow more distinct. My insides get tighter and my mood darker.

The tableau that greets me in the dining room, a room of heavy mahogany furniture as old-fashioned as the stuff in the parlor, has all the appeal of a scene in a Broadway show with a lousy script. Two people sit at the big dining table. A third is standing near, a newspaper under his arm. The table is so highly polished it reflects their faces along with the flowery porcelain teapot, the matching teacups, and the silver tray of honey cake. Two of the guests look surprised. The third is stoic, seated in his dining chair, looking at me with no particular expression but threatening nonetheless. But Sig Loreale is always stoic and always threatening.

Of the other two guests, the ones with surprised looks, the one standing—his overcoat a color that can't make up its mind between drab brown and even drabber gray, his fedora pushed back on his head—is someone I'd never expect would ever be welcome in Mom Sheinbaum's house: a cop, specifically the stockily built sergeant with a tough-as-nails face, Liam Adair of the New York City Police Department. As cops go, Adair is one of the less crummy ones. As far as I'm aware, he's not on the take, doesn't plant evidence, and doesn't beat people up too often. He plays things pretty square, at least as square as he can in the blue fraternity's code of silence. Still, he'd love to put me away any chance he gets, and he's always looking for the chance.

The other surprise guest isn't really out of place in Mom's

house; it's just the timing that flummoxes me. It doesn't shock me that Lily and Mom know each other. Hell, they've probably done business together. But seeing Lily here now, after Nick's murder, after Sig's warning to me to stay out of anything connected to Nick's death or his clandestine arrangement with Abby, and after I've lusted after Lily all day today, throws me for a loop that threatens to strangle me.

Mom takes her place at the head of the table. "Come, have some tea and honey cake, Cantor," she says in her sing-song that's deceptively warmhearted. "It'll calm you."

Lily says, "I think Cantor might prefer a drink." She gets up from her chair. The pleated skirt of her black knit dress brushes her legs just below her knees and sways gently along her hips as she walks to the sideboard to pour me a drink. The sight of her, of her short, windblown-style blond hair that tempts my fingers, and the way that dress fits snug upstairs and sways below, triggers memories of last night in her hotel, memories which could get in my way of dealing with this unsettling tableau of an unexpected gathering. I squelch the memories, strain to keep them squelched when Lily hands me a glass of scotch and her fingers brush mine.

She sits down again.

I take a seat at the other end of the table. I don't dare sit next to Lily, and certainly not next to Sig, who's the only one not looking at me. I'm about to start peppering everyone with questions when Adair takes the newspaper from under his arm and slides it across the table. It's this morning's *Daily News,* which I hadn't seen. The enormous all-caps headline is a punch to the gut: BIG TIME BOOKIE DEAD. The photo beneath the headline hits me even harder: Nick broken and bleeding on the Bronx sidewalk, the hard flash of the news photographer's camera glinting on the glass shards all over and around Nick's body. The glass glitters like gaudy insults to Nick's last moments of life.

I look over at Sig, who's still not looking at me. He's sipping his tea, his lips pressed tight. It's the only hint that underneath his stoic exterior he's annoyed.

There could be only two reasons why Nick's killing wound up in the paper, since Sig usually controls what gets into the news and what doesn't, and what the cops either pursue or ignore if he wants them to. One reason is maybe he's decided to have the story splashed on the front page to draw out the killer who's dared to do away with one of Sig's business associates. But I get the feeling it's the other reason, the one causing Sig's barely concealed irritation: someone else made sure the cops and the news hounds were all over Nick's murder. Someone who wanted to get Sig's attention and send the message that Sig might not be operating in the impregnable fortress he and everyone else thinks he is, someone like the mysterious operator Nick said wanted to move in on Sig and squeeze him out.

Adair nods to the newspaper on the table. "Word has it you were friends with Fortunato. But I suppose you know nothing about this, Gold?" he says with enough sarcasm to peel the wallpaper.

I give him my soul-of-cooperation smile. "Sure, I can tell you a few things about it, sergeant," I say.

"Lieutenant," he says.

"Oh? I hadn't heard. Well, congratulations, *lieutenant*," I say. "Nice to know the police department recognizes talent when they see it. But okay, sure, about Nick's killing, I can tell you things maybe you already know. Things like I went to Nick's apartment yesterday evening to celebrate his birthday, something I do every year. Things like he wasn't home. Things like he was holed up in a crummy hotel in the Bronx—" I hold back from glancing at Sig—"and that I was on the street when Nick crashed to the pavement." I sip my scotch while I look around the table at the assembly of faces. "But what I'd like to know is what can any of you tell *me* about it? I want Nick's killer found. I want whoever did it—" I break off and give Adair a chilly smile before finishing—"to meet justice. That's why I'm here, to see if Mrs. Sheinbaum can get a line on any word on the street about Nick's killing. Now, the question is, why are all of *you* here? Is it about Nick's murder? And since when do two of the Law's prime targets, Sig Loreale and Esther Sheinbaum, share a chummy afternoon of tea and honey cake with a sterling member of the police department? Never, that's when. Because now that I think about it, Nick's murder has nothing to do with this little gathering, or at least it didn't to begin with. Miss Vardanian's presence here seals it. It's Miss Vardanian's talents you want, Sig, or maybe Mom, or maybe both of you, right? And with the blessing of the New York City Police Department in the person of Lieutenant Liam Adair?"

Sig looks at me as he pushes the newspaper away with the nonchalance of someone whose cleaning lady overlooked a bit of dust. "Mr. Fortunato's death complicates matters, Cantor," he says in his slow, gravel-voiced way, intimidation lurking as much between his words as in them. "As does your presence here."

"Why?" The little word shoots through the room.

It's squashed by a teeth-gnashing scrape of a fork against a plate. It's Mom Sheinbaum scraping up the last crumbs of her honey cake. "*Bubbeleh*," she says, "you shouldn't ask so many questions. What's one bookie's killing nowadays? Nicky Fast Hands wasn't the only bookie in town. Okay, sure, he was a nice guy, a real *mensch*, and he knew his business. But he knew the risks of the game. And so do you, Cantor."

Funny, how people like Mom and Sig demand loyalty of everyone they deal with but offer none of it in return. To Sig, Nick was just another source of profit, his murder an irritating hindrance to whatever he's got going on with the people in this room. At least Mom admitted that Nick was a *mensch*, a human being. But an expendable one.

He wasn't expendable to me.

I notice that Adair is a little fidgety and trying to hide it. "What's wrong, Lieutenant? You look like you've got the itches, like maybe you're allergic to something. Maybe you've got a cop's allergies to letting a murder go unsolved? And since when do you willingly do business with the likes of the criminal crowd around this table?"

These aren't questions he'll satisfy with an answer. I have to look elsewhere, to someone maybe more sympathetic to ideals of trust and loyalty, the kind of trust she gave me under my hands last night.

Warmed by the glow of our tryst, I say, "Tell me, Lily, whose pocket do they want you to pick? Whose briefcase do they want you to purloin? What could possibly benefit the machinations of Mr. Loreale or Mom Sheinbaum and the needs of the New York City Police Department?"

The silence around the table is so heavy it could crush stone.

But Lily smiles at me, a slow smile that meanders through the heavy atmosphere like a cat walking on silent paws. "Cantor, nobody here wants you to get hurt—"

Lieutenant Adair cuts in, "Don't expect the police department to cry over it, though."

"All right, then," Lily continues, "*I* don't want you to get hurt. Really, I don't."

"I can take care of myself," I say.

"I know you can. But sometimes situations are bigger and more dangerous than you can handle."

"Is that so? How do you know I can't handle whatever situation all of you are cooking up until I see it for myself? And what the hell does whatever you're cooking up have to do with Nick's killing? Or the unknown somebody who's threatening to move in on Sig? Oh, didn't you know?" I don't need Sig's quick, almost imperceptible tightening of his jowly jaw to keep me from spilling the beans about the dead thug Sig arranged to have quietly removed from Nick's apartment. I make it a practice not to discuss such goings-on when there's a cop in the room. Sig finally turns to look at me, silently studying me as if I'm a pest crawling across a picnic lunch. "Cantor," he says my name so slowly and quietly it's nearly under his breath, "Mr. Fortunato's death has nothing at all to do with our business here, except the newspaper's attention to it complicates matters. And whether you choose to believe it or not, I am in agreement with Miss Vardanian; I have no wish to see you harmed. But if you persist in pursuing the matter of Mr. Fortunato's death, you will find yourself in great danger, a danger I might not be able to assist you in avoiding."

In other words, his business with this cabal around Mom's table is more important than my life. No surprise. Sig's businesses, his pursuit of power, have always been more important to him than anyone's life, even when he was a young upstart muscling his way into the rackets in Coney Island. Bodies turned up under the boardwalk, in pieces in the lockers of the bathhouses, in the Tunnel of Love's boats and the Cyclone's rollercoaster seats. Sig took over Coney Island the way he eventually took over the rest of New York, except now there's no blood on his shirts. He pays people to bloody their own shirts to get rid of anyone in Sig's way, people of no importance to him.

Well, there was one person whose life was important to Sig. Hard to believe he was actually in love once. But life with Sig Loreale is a dangerous deal, and the woman was murdered on their wedding night by a traitor in Sig's organization. Sig's never allowed love into his life ever since. He sealed off that part of himself in steel and stone.

I hate having anything in common with the guy, but I know how he feels. I was in love once, too, deeply in love with a woman who not only brought excitement into my bed but tenderness into my rough life. Her name was Sophie, Sophie de la Lune y Sol, my Sophie of the Moon and the Sun. But life with me, like life with Sig Loreale, is a dangerous deal, and I saw her go down in a hail of bullets on a tropical street. I couldn't get to her in time to save her. It still haunts me.

Sig's unfortunate bride was Mom Sheinbaum's daughter. Mom's never forgiven Sig for putting her precious daughter in danger. But Mom still does business with him, because business is business.

Like whatever business is going on among the criminal big-timers around this table.

So why is Lieutenant Adair here? But Abby O'Neill isn't?

It's time to rattle the cages, see what falls out, and if any of it has Nick's name on it. "So, Sig, how's the deal with Abby progressing? I stopped by her place for coffee this morning. Did she mention it? Her coffee packed quite a punch. And oh, Chickie D'Andrea was there, too. I didn't know they were close. Did you?"

Sig picks up his teacup, takes a sip, then puts it down so slowly, so quietly, it barely taps the saucer. He never looks at me. "Lieutenant Adair," he finally says, "please escort Cantor out of the house."

We're halfway through the parlor when Adair finally lets go of my arm.

I say, "Aren't you taking a big chance, lieutenant, trusting that I'll just leave? How do you know I won't walk right back into the dining room and keep pestering everyone until I get what I want?"

"Because you're smart enough to know it won't do you any good. No one will tell you anything, Gold."

"True," I say. I take a good look at Adair. He looks about as comfortable with his assignment as a dog straining on a leash. "What's happened to you, Adair? You always hated Loreale. You've wanted to put him behind bars even more than you want to put me away. Since when did you become just another of Loreale's lackey cops?"

His eyes darken and shrink to slits in his tough face, all muscle and rough skin. Looking at him is like watching an animal who's spotted prey. I'm the prey.

I step back from him, a move of sheer, involuntary instinct.

He says, "Whatever's between me and Loreale is none of your business. But here's something that's *my* business. Police business. That line you gave about someone trying to move in on Loreale? Where'd you get that, Gold? From Fortunato? And why do you think it ties into Fortunato's killing?" He practically barks it.

"Take it easy," I say. I pull out my pack of Chesterfields and my lighter, and shake out a coupled of smokes. "Want one?"

"Save the good manners act," he says. "Just tell me what you meant about someone tightening the screws on Loreale and how maybe it's got something to do with Fortunato's killing."

"You know the game, lieutenant," I say, and light my smoke. "You don't get something for nothing. If you want to get, you have to give. Let's start with the easy stuff. Who tipped the police about Nick's murder, and who planted the story and picture in the paper? Was it Loreale?"

His chuckle is so full of bite I'm surprised his tongue's not bleeding. "What makes you think I'd help you, Gold?"

"Because I think you're an honest cop who doesn't like unanswered questions or answers that conveniently get lost. At least, you used to be an honest cop. The company you're currently keeping," I say with a nod toward the dining room, "suggests otherwise. What's going on with you, Adair? Tired of the nickels and dimes of a cop's pay?"

"You know what, Gold?" he says so calmly he's barely breathing. "I ought to slap you around for that remark. But I won't even give it that much dignity."

"All right, my apologies," I say. "Glad to hear that your

shield's still clean and shiny. So, since you're an honest cop, how about we get back to a little tit for tat for information, and you give me honest answers?"

Adair's cynical chuckle dissolves into one of those deep, thoughtful breaths that tells me that his soul really does live on the up-and-up. He lets the breath out, says, "Okay, I'll give you this one, Gold, but first you give me whatever you've got, or it's no deal. Who's moving in on Loreale, and how do you know?"

A deep pull on my smoke gives me a moment to tumble the deal in my mind. If it was any other cop, I'd tell him to go dig up the information for himself and jump in the hole while he's at it. But if Adair is as good as his word, and he still plays square, and if I get information in return that helps me find Nick's killer, it's a game worth playing. "I don't know who's moving in on Sig," I say, "but yeah, I got it from Nick. Some punk showed up at his place to muscle Nick out of his bookie business. The guy told Nick that Loreale's time was over, too."

"Who was the punk? And where is he now?"

"Uh-uh, lieutenant," I say, blowing more smoke. I'm not about to share with a cop, even an honest cop, that Nick killed the guy in a struggle and Sig arranged for the disposal of the body. "A deal's a deal," I remind Adair. "It's your turn to fork over. Who tipped the police about Nick's murder, and who planted the story and picture in the paper? Loreale?"

"I'm not sure." He gives it a shrug, follows it with a thinking man's tight lips, then says, "But it wouldn't surprise me."

"To maybe draw out the killer?" I say.

"I imagine that would be the idea. Okay, your turn again, Gold. I guess you figure that whoever it is that's trying to muscle Sig is responsible for Fortunato's death?"

"It fits, don't you think? At least for now."

"What do you mean 'for now'?"

"I mean maybe it has to do with whatever the hell's going on with that crowd in the dining room. Why is a cop doing business with that bunch? What's Lily Vardanian been recruited to do? And why does everybody want me to walk away from Nick's killing?"

"You've run out of your allotted questions, Gold. Now just get the hell outta here."

Chapter Thirteen

By the time I park my car down the street from my apartment, I've tumbled though various moods since being summarily dismissed from Mom's place: anger, confusion, disgust, frustration, but sadness most of all. It hurts like hell that Nick's murder is being treated as nothing more than an annoyance.

I get it: life is often cheap in the criminal world I share with Sig and Mom and even Lily. The same could be said for Adair's world, where the dead might wind up as mere statistics on a police blotter. But even in our hard worlds where life is cheap, cheap is at least something. Cheap is better than worthless.

I won't let Nick's life be worthless. I know what that's like. There isn't a week that goes by that I don't have to face down the twitching fists of some bigot who considers me scum for the way I live my life and who I choose to love. My life isn't merely cheap in their eyes, it's worthless.

For that matter, the life of the punk who threatened Nick and who wound up dead himself shouldn't be worthless, either. He must've mattered to somebody, even if it was just whoever it was that sent him to muscle Nick in the first place.

If I knew who the punk was, I might be able to trace a line to who sent him, who's behind his threat to move in on Sig.

And if I knew who was behind him, I might have a line on who killed Nick.

But I'll never find the punk. He's probably in bits and pieces by now, fragments of flesh and bone thrown in the river or as far away as the New Jersey swamps. Sig's henchmen are good at their jobs.

Nick's death and how it's being tossed aside like yesterday's trash isn't the only thing breaking my heart. Knowing that Lily is part of the secret shenanigans Sig and Mom and Adair are concocting is twisting me up. I figured last night that she's here in New York on a job. I just never figured the job would crash into my life.

But it has, and as I walk from my car to my apartment building, I wonder what I'm going to do about it.

My mood improves a little in the welcoming familiarity of the early evening dusk settling over my street. The neighborhood's lights are coming on. The circular glow of streetlights dot the sidewalk and slide across men's caps and fedoras and women's colorful little hats as their wearers hurry along. Neon lights from the signs and marquees on the nearby nightclubs and theaters throw color across the neighborhood and the faces of everyone on the street. Lights are on in apartments where people are home from work or getting dinner ready, busy living life. For the first time since leaving Mom's place, where my presence was clearly not wanted, I feel like I belong.

"Cantor! Hey, Cantor!"

I turn toward of the sound of my name.

It's Mike Landers.

He's cleaned up and sobered up since I saw him this morning. He's getting out of his car, a late model black-and-coral Pontiac sedan, tarted up even more with too much chrome, which looks even gaudier under a streetlamp. I didn't think Mike was the type for flashy cars, especially since seeing the nondescript furnishings he surrounds himself with in his apartment, but I guess you never know what makes people happy. He's certainly not a flashy dresser. His dark gray overcoat hangs straight as a board on his wiry frame. His gray fedora looks bigger than it should above his thin face.

I say, "What brings you around, Mike? You get over your jitters about someone coming after you?"

The sudden crinkling of his eyes tells me I'm wrong, and that he's still a nervous pup. "I gotta talk to you, Cantor," he says. "I knocked on your apartment door, but when there was no answer I figured you weren't home, so I took a chance you'd show up sooner or later. I just waited in my car."

"Sooner or later's a big chance to take. What if I didn't come home 'til midnight?"

"I'd have waited. It's important, Cantor."

It must be, or Mike Landers, alumnus of the city's dockside streets, survivor of Big Bill McGraw's old waterfront mob, wouldn't be the Nervous Nellie holding on to the door handle of his car for support, or maybe for a fast escape. "Okay, Mike," I say, "c'mon up. You can tell me what's on your mind."

He takes my arm. "No, there's something I gotta show you, someplace I gotta take you. Come on, get in my car. I'll drive."

I'm not crazy about being hustled into someone's car without knowing where we're going and why. I yank my arm away, but Mike's still got a piece of my coat sleeve. I pull that away from him, too. "I'm not going anywhere with you until you tell me what the hell is going on."

"I'll explain everything when we get there," he says, tugging at me again.

I pull myself away, but I've got no chance to bolt because someone else gets out of the car, and another set of hands— Freddie Holmes's hands—grab hold of me. Together, Freddie and Mike push me into the back seat of Mike's Pontiac.

We head across town to the East Side, a stop-and-go ordeal in the last crush of rush-hour traffic. It was dusk when we left my neighborhood. It's nighttime now. Pedestrians on the clogged sidewalks are making better time than Mike's Pontiac.

With Mike driving and Freddie beside him in the passenger's seat, neither are holding a gun on me. I can get out any time, like now, when Mike's car is boxed in by a big-finned green-and-white Dodge in front, its round red tail lights staring at us, and an impatient horn-honking yellow cab behind, its headlights illuminating the backs of Mike's and Freddie's heads. But I stay put, my curiosity getting the better of me, and I stick with whatever adventure Mike and Freddie have in mind. I even try to make conversation, get the fellas to fill me in on why they want me to go wherever the hell it is we're going. All I get is, "You'll see," from Mike as he navigates the traffic tie-up. Freddie offers just small nods, his gray cap barely moving. We eventually get free of the worst of the traffic as Queens-bound cars veer off for the approach to the 59th Street Bridge. Mike takes a right turn on Second Avenue, a somewhat more well-heeled stretch than in Mom Sheinbaum's downtown neighborhood. He eventually takes a left and drives to a corner of Beekman Place, one of the fancier blocks backing up to the East River in an already diamond-studded neighborhood.

"Who's the fat cat we're we going to see?" I say.

Freddie says, "It ain't a who. It's a what," just as Mike pulls into a service alley next to an apartment building whose fancy entrance looks like it would be just as comfortable in sixteenth-century Renaissance Venice as in 1958 New York. The shadowy glow of streetlamps and the watery reflections of the East River only increase the mood.

"We're here," Mike says.

We three get out of the Pontiac. The alley's dark except for a naked lightbulb above the steel door of the building's service entrance. The bulb's glare makes the three of us look dead.

Mike takes a small ring of keys from his pocket and unlocks the service door.

Inside, he slips a ten dollar bill to a guy in a gray denim janitor's getup. The guy nods and goes about his business organizing garbage cans.

Freddie and I follow Mike past the janitor's area to a hallway that branches off in two directions. The one to the right probably leads to the lobby for deliveries to the apartment building. The one to the left is a short hall ending in a door. We take the left hall. Mike opens the door.

With Freddie in front of me and Mike behind, we walk down a dimly lit concrete stairway. Another door at the bottom of the stairs brings us into the building's garage.

If the pricey cars parked in all the spaces are any indication of who lives in the apartments upstairs, it's a good bet that those apartments are decked out in the fanciest of everything. There are plenty of sleek Cadillacs and the latest sharp-angled Lincolns for the new-money crowd, sporty foreign jobs for the jet set, and Rolls Royces and Bentleys that occupy their spaces like royalty waiting for obeisance. Evidently they all enter and leave the place through what I'd guess is one of those new automatic garage doors on a far wall that likely leads to a ramp to the street.

I should look into doing a little business here, see if anyone needs an extra Michaelangelo or Titian for an empty spot on their wall.

"This way," Mike says, leading us to a padlocked, sliding metal door marked No Entry. He selects another key from the key ring, unlocks the door, slides it open, and closes it behind us as we go down another set of stairs.

Neither Mike nor Freddie have given me any indication up to now that they want to put the strangle on me, knock me out, or worse, put holes in me with a knife or gun. But the deeper we go down below the building, the air growing gritty with decades-old dust and musty with equally old secrets, my skin gets clammy as my flight-or-fight reflex kicks in.

In the near darkness of the stairway, no one sees me slide my hand under my coat and into my suit jacket and come to rest on the butt of my gun.

We must've come to another door. I hear it open and feel a slight draft as Mike, who's in front of me, opens it. Inside, we're in pitch dark until either Mike or Freddie, I can't see which, finds a switch next to the door and turns the lights on.

I feel like we've stepped out of time. Glass-globed lamps hanging on ornate brass chains suspended from the high, arched ceiling have the same Renaissance feel as the entrance to the apartment building. The lamps send an antique glow through the large room, about the same size as the garage. The brick-lined walls are a warm red-brown, accented here and there with arched articulations in keeping with the apartment building's Italian Renaissance getup. Small round tables, some still with dust-encrusted white tablecloths, are scattered around the room. A few tables even have long-empty glasses on them. Several chairs are overturned. There's a black-walnut bar with a mirrored top along one wall, and a large open door in an adjacent wall. It's a real door but that section of wall isn't: the door's camouflaged by the same brick that surrounds the room. When the door's closed, you'd never see it, just like all good escape routes.

I turn around to get the full scope of the place. It could be only one thing: an abandoned speakeasy, the kind of watering hole that catered to monied imbibers of the 1920s. I give the place an appreciative whistle. "This must've been where the swells did their drinking," I say, and indulge in a vision of satin-gowned women swooshing through the joint on the arms of tuxedoed millionaire Wall Streeters or the deep-pocketed gangsters who probably owned the place. Lucky Luciano might've tossed back a few here, toasting a recent illicit cash haul masterminded by his numbers-savvy pal Meyer Lansky. Maybe even Sig himself dropped in here to rub elbows with his betters while he was still a young hustler skimming the rackets in Coney Island.

Sig.

My pleasant daydream of yesteryear's glamour girls and gangsters fades away, replaced by the chill of a current possibility. "Does Sig know about this place?" I say.

"Beats me," Mike says. He takes his hat off, runs his hand through his hair, opens his coat and suit jacket and sits down at one of the tables. His long, thin frame folds itself into the chair like a worn-out set of pleats. His .45, the same one he held in his lap this morning when he was drunk with whiskey and fear, is visible under his arm through his open coat and jacket.

I get that jittery feeling again.

I open my coat and sit down opposite Mike. Freddie rights an overturned chair and joins us. He takes his cap off, puts it on the table, but keeps hold of it, clutching it like it's an anchor to a safe harbor. He looks like he'd rather be anywhere else in the world than here, but can't be.

I say, "What are we doing here, fellas?"

Mike says, "Listen, Cantor, if Loreale knows about this place, then whatever he and Abby's got planned is bigger than just reopening Nick's bookie operation. But if Loreale doesn't know about the place, then Abby's playing a dangerous game by operating on her own. If that's what she's doing, she's putting the crew in danger, too; that is, if she really intends to keep us on, which I guess she does because she showed me the place this afternoon and gave me the keys so I could start getting phone lines in. I guess she wants to start making book as soon as possible."

An icy cold runs through me, the kind that bites when the air in the room is suddenly infected with something sinister. "Nick's not even been dead twenty-four hours," I say, "and already Abby's setting up shop?"

I look around again. If it's going to be a bookie spot, it'll be the classiest betting parlor this side of Monte Carlo. It's certainly in the right neighborhood. Lots of money around here and not far from its cousins along Park and Fifth Avenues and all the townhouse- and mansion-lined streets in between.

It's awfully big for a bookie joint.

Abby certainly has big dreams, which doesn't surprise me. If she's sharing those dreams with Sig, that doesn't surprise me, either. But if she's dreaming alone, that's surprising the hell out of me, though the idea of a woman grabbing power is deliciously sexy.

I say, "Why did you guys bring me here? What's any of this got to do with me?"

Freddie sits up fast and straight, his eyes blazing. "Somethin' is very wrong with all of this, Cantor," he says, waving an arm around the room. "An' somethin' tells me that whatever it is that's wrong has somethin' to do with Nick's murder, an' you seem to be the only one who gives a damn about that. So look aroun' Cantor. Somethin' is *wrong*."

I take Freddie's advice and look around again. I look at the walls, the hidden door, the fancy lamps, the bar, and as I take it all in, looking for anything that has anything to do with Nick's death, Mike says, "How many bookie joints you been in, Cantor?"

"A fair number," I say. "Why?"

"Ever see any this big?"

"Can't say that I have."

"Something tells me that this place is gonna be more than a bookie parlor," Mike says.

"Okay, sure, why not," I say, still looking around. "A casino? Lots of room for gaming tables. Or some sort of nightclub? The place is big enough for a beauty of a floor show."

Mike's *tsk* rings sharp in the big, empty room. "Nick never wanted anything this fancy," he says.

"Oh, I don't know," I say. "Nick had a classy side to him."

"Classy, sure. But he wasn't one to dig too deep into his pockets. Listen, one night about a month ago when I walked into the office to give Nick the last hour's betting slips, I caught Abby arguing with Nick, telling him it was time to expand the operation, take in more cash, but Nick wasn't going for it."

That gets my attention. I stop looking around the room and look directly at Mike. "That doesn't sound like Nick," I say. "I knew him all my life, saw him start with a handful of Coney Island sand and go on to run the most profitable bookie joint in New York. Even as a kid, Nick was always looking for more ways to rake in cash. What stopped him this time?"

"Smarts," Freddie says with admiration.

Mike says, "The operation was making money hand over fist. We were taking in so much dough Nick could afford to pay everyone on the crew real good, give the cops their steady payoff, give Loreale his regular cut, and still make his profit. And as far as I know, Loreale was happy with Nick's way of doing business. Sure, Abby knew every dime that came in and out; that was part of her job. But so did Nick. And he worked lean."

Freddie slaps the table, points a finger at me and says, "An' that's the best way to run a bookie joint, lean. It's the way I ran my joint up in Harlem. Sure, the place can be real nice, with a good supply of booze for the in-house bettors, an' give 'em chairs that are real comfy. But no fancy frills, like a big joint to pay big rent for and that you gotta heat up in winter and cool down in summer. Y'know what it would take to turn a profit on a place this big? Even if it's more than just a bettin' parlor? Now, sure, maybe Nick could do it, he had a good head for operatin', but I doubt he'd want to shell out what it's gonna take to get this place up and runnin'. So where's *Miss Abby* gettin' the money?"

I keep it to myself that I saw Abby meet with Sig at his penthouse last night. I make it a practice to keep whatever's between me and Sig to stay between me and Sig. I just say, "I assume Loreale's going into business with her, just like he did with Nick when Nick started out."

Mike shakes his head slowly, like he's thinking things over, trying to figure things out. He sucks in a deep breath that causes his skinny face to look positively skeletal. After he blows the breath out, filling his cheeks so that I know he's alive, he says, "I know you know Loreale better than I do, Cantor. I know you two go way back to when you and Nick were kids. But Freddie and I know the day-to-day business he did with Nick"—I notice Freddie nodding in agreement— "and I'm sure Freddie would agree with me that Sig Loreale and Nick Fortunato were two of a kind when it came to business. Loreale doesn't spend a penny he doesn't have to. He was getting his cut from Nick's business real smooth, no extra expenses, no hiccups in the payoffs to the cops. So okay, sure, maybe he's going into business with Abby. But maybe he isn't. If he is, the only way the two of them could make a deal is if Nick is out of the way. And if Loreale isn't backing Abby, well, I wouldn't put it past Abby to clear her own path, if you know what I mean."

I know what he means, and yeah, the idea has crossed my mind.

But if that's the case, there's still Freddie's question: if the seed money's not from Sig, where's Abby getting the cash?

The door opens, and two guns come out fast from under two coats: my .38 and Mike's .45. Two guns get put away again when Abby walks through the door.

Mike's face has gone white as bleached bones, Freddie's face has gone ashy, and I'm the only one of the three of us who's smiling. I'm smiling because Abby O'Neill, sashaying into the room in a belted red wool coat, black leather gloves, red high-heeled shoes, carrying a black clutch bag under her arm, and looking at the three of us like we're items on a cheap menu, is the sort of sight that makes various parts of me positively tingle.

And no, I haven't forgotten that she drugged me this morning, but I can hold two ideas in my head at the same time: that she's dangerous and that she looks terrific in red.

She unties the belt and opens her coat, revealing a high-necked black knit sheath dress that more or less makes love to her body from her neck to just below her knees. Distracted by the action of that dress, it takes me a minute to realize that she's not alone. Chickie is with her.

Chubby Chickie in a shapeless brown overcoat, the usual tuft of his crewcut sticking out from under his dull brown fedora, is quite the contrast to svelte Abby. Even their smiles are at odds. Hers is cunning. His is comic, the smile of a guy trying too hard to be savvy and tough.

Abby slides her gloves off, brushes her hand through her dark hair, narrows her eyes, but keeps smiling, her creamy red lipstick catching a glint of light. "Is this a private party?" she purrs. "Or can anyone join?"

There's a chair nearby, I pull it over for her. Chickie can get his own damn chair.

He doesn't bother, just stands obediently behind Abby when she sits down. His slightly bulgy eyes look the rest of us over, looking for any sign that we might intrude on his territory.

Abby says, "Well, Mike, how are you doing with getting the telephone lines in?"

"The lines are going in tomorrow."

"Good," she says. "And you understand I want the phone lines for the call-in bets over there along that back wall? And then a separate line over here in this corner"—she nods toward the corner beyond the entry door—"and another behind the bar," she finishes with a sweep of her arm toward the bar. "Those two lines will have different telephone exchanges than the betting lines."

"Sure. That's the plan," Mike says.

She turns to Freddie. "Always nice to see you, Freddie," she says. "Please say hello to your wife for me."

"Thank you, Miss Abby," he says. "My Ida will be glad you asked after her."

"You're lucky to have her, Freddie. Ida is a treasure. But now, please explain to me why you're here with Mike and Cantor."

Freddie's fingering his cap again. He keeps his eyes on what he's doing, careful not to look at the white lady who, for the moment at least, is still his boss. Freddie knew that Nick didn't give a damn about the color of his skin, just the smarts in Freddie's brain. But according to the story Freddie told me earlier today at his place, Abby made it painfully clear that she didn't share the same enlightened attitude. Respectfully, but with a subtle pride that refuses to be timid, he says, "Thought I'd give Mike a hand. Y'know, help him measure out the phone connections, make fast work of it."

Abby gives him a smile that appears to be genuine, but right now everything about Abby, including her smiles, is suspect in my book, probably in Freddie's, too.

She turns her smile on me. It's not a particularly warm one but it's not entirely unfriendly, either. It's what you might call a teasing smile. "Actually, I'm more interested in why Cantor is here," she says. "It seems you don't pay attention to warnings, Cantor, which is too bad. Haven't I told you I've always liked you?"

If words and a sultry voice could stroke a cheek, hers just did. Or maybe she scratched me with her fingernails, and I just don't know the difference.

"So you keep telling me," I say. "I have to admit, your affection could be fun but the risk might be too dangerous."

"Since when has a little danger ever stopped you, Cantor? It's one of the things I like about you, your willingness to defy a world that wants to silence you, your insistence to live life your own way. I find that a very attractive quality, as attractive as the good taste you have in clothes. That brown suit and lovely pale green shirt look wonderful on you."

It's moments like this, when Abby is trying to play me in ways she's smart enough to figure I might like being played, that I have to keep in mind that Nick trusted her, and Nick was no fool. "And what about you, Abby? How many people would you defy to get what you want?"

"What makes you think I'd have to defy anyone?"

There's that chill again. If Abby's signaling me that she's not going behind Sig's back or defying him by setting up a business in this place—whatever the business is—then what they're planning must've been in the works even before Nick died.

I'm thinking a thought I'd rather not think, a thought too ugly to pin on a woman as beautiful as Abby: I'm wondering if Abby might be the so-called employer who sent the thug to put the squeeze on Nick.

But that thought is part of a puzzle with all the wrong pieces, since the thug threatened to muscle Sig out, too. And if that meeting at Sig's last night was anything to go by, Abby's in league with Sig, not against him. But as I said, everything about Abby is iffy now, especially her loyalties, if she ever had any.

I say, "I guess you wouldn't have to defy anyone. So tell me, Abby, just what do you have in mind for this place?" I leave Sig's name out of it. It's not for me to spill the beans, especially when I don't know what kind of beans they are.

Abby gives me a wink that signals she appreciates me keeping my mouth shut. "Oh, something rather special," she says. "There'll be a betting operation, certainly, but with a much better cover than simply paying off the police to look the other way. A rather elegant cover, I must say. And a profitable one."

"Is that so? You're going into the elegance business? If you're planning to keep Chickie on your payroll, you'd better get him a better tailor."

That gets a chuckle from Mike, even from Freddie. In all my years of seeing them at Nick's bookie joint, it's the first indication that maybe they're not too nuts about the guy. Can't blame them.

Chickie, of course, isn't laughing. "Maybe I oughtta use your tailor, Cantor," he says, his foggy voice shot through with resentment. "Your tailor might be relieved to finally measure an inseam he's familiar with." He finishes it with a snicker.

Mike and Freddie start to chuckle again but after a glance at me they think better of it. Good for them.

I take out my pack of smokes and lighter, offer a smoke to Abby, who takes it. She brings her face close and keeps her eyes on me when I light her smoke. Her eyes glitter in the flame.

She pulls away, takes a deep drag, blows it past my shoulder.

I light my own smoke and say, "Just what kind of joint are you planning here, Abby? What sort of elegant spot would cover a bookie joint? The place is certainly big enough to divvy up, conceal the bookie operation. A little earlier I threw around the idea of maybe a nightclub, maybe a supper club. You'd look swell greeting the customers. There isn't a satin gown that wouldn't enjoy sliding along your body."

Abby gives that a smile that's flattered, wary, shrewd, amused, and annoyed all at the same time. "I've always known you're smart, Cantor," she says with an undertone that maybe I'm too smart for my own good. "Well, you're right. I'm opening a supper club. Music, floor show, dancing, the works, in an elegant room."

"And no one," I say, "not even cops, will ever know there's a bookie joint behind a false wall."

"Quite," Abby says.

"They'd better not know about it," I say, "or you'll never get your liquor license or cabaret license."

I don't think I've ever seen a more dismissive look in a woman's eyes, and I've seen women's eyes cut me to the knees.

"Don't be ridiculous," Abby says so quietly I read it more on her lips than hear her say it.

Of course. The licenses are already in the bag. What usually takes the owner of a new saloon or nightclub months to get after filling out enough paperwork to give you hand cramp, either Abby's old Irish mob connections, or Sig, if he's in on this, can take care of with an arm twist or a phone call.

Abby's smiling at me again. My stupidity, if not forgotten, is at least dismissed. "And besides," she says, "That's why I've hired the best architect in town for the legit part of the operation. He'll never see the bookie set-up behind a new wall, won't even know it's there. But the club will be beautiful, very classy. I'll have notices in the finest magazines and the entertainment columns. Everyone who's anyone will want to be here, and so will everyone who wants to be anyone. You know as well as I do, Cantor, the city is flooded with money these days. This neighborhood alone is soaking in it, plus all that restless cash in the pockets and bank accounts of all those people in all those new suburbs and from all over the country who come to the big city for a little sophisticated fun. That's the American Dream, isn't it? Make enough money to spend on a big house, a big car, and a night of big fun? Isn't that your American Dream, Cantor?"

"Not all of it," I say.

"Why Cantor, I didn't realize you could be so greedy. What more do you want?"

"What more do I want?" I lean back in my chair, take a drag on my smoke, keep my eyes on Abby. "How about this for an American Dream? How about you welcome me as a customer here. How about you think it's honky-dory for me to take my place on the dance floor with a woman who thinks I'm swell. How about you even dance with me?"

The expressions on everyone's faces suddenly freeze: Mike looks like he's heard a foreign language he doesn't understand; Freddie, his face gone bland and guarded, looks at his hat; Chickie sneers; and Abby's smile is so hard I expect her lipstick to crack. She finally says, "I hear there are places where you and your . . . well, lady friends are quite welcome, Cantor."

"And I'd be happy to take you there any time you'd like. I bet you can dance up a storm."

I can feel Mike and Freddy growing more uncomfortable by the second. Abby, though, doesn't even twitch. "I'm afraid I'll be too busy running this place," she says.

"Well, the offer's always open," I say. "What are you planning to call this joint?"

Everyone's face relaxes. Everyone's glad I changed the subject.

After a deep drag on her smoke, Abby gives me a friendlier if sly smile. "I don't know yet. Any suggestions?"

I take another a pull on my smoke, blow it out and give Abby a smile as sly as hers. "How about, Nick's Heavenly Rest? You know, in honor of the guy who set you up in the bookie racket in the first place."

Abby's fingers tighten on her cigarette. She looks around for an ashtray. Realizing there aren't any, she drops her smoke to the floor, crushes it out hard with the toe of her shoe. "It's time you got off it, Cantor," she says, her voice, usually smooth and sultry, now deep and rough. "Nick is dead and gone. It's tragic, but life goes on. Why are you doing this? What was Nick to you? I know he wasn't your amour. Your eyes follow skirts. So what was Nick to you?"

"A friend!" I say, so angry I growl it, making Abby shrink back from me a little. "Nick was my friend. Isn't that enough? Or don't you have any idea what that means. Do you have any friends, Abby? Does anyone give a damn about you?"

"She's got me," Chickie says.

As angry as I was a few seconds ago, that's how much pity I feel now. Chickie D'Andrea, the odds guy, the guy who can spot bad numbers a mile away, can't see the bad odds stacked against his deluded hopes right in front of him. It's a good thing he's standing behind Abby, or he'd see the smirk crawl across her mouth.

I've had enough. I've had enough of Abby's hard heart, of Chickie's sniveling worship, of Mike's and Freddie's obedience.

I crush my own smoke on the floor, get up from the table. On my way to the door, I say, "Let me know when you decide what to call this place. And make sure you spell Nick's name right."

Chapter Fourteen

If I was poison to the crowd at Mom's place, or to Abby and her grand schemes, their irritation with me pales in comparison to the hostility right in my face when I walk into the midtown police station.

I open my coat in the heat of the stuffy squad room, which only invites additional stares from the boys in blue. Some of the stares ride on sneers, some with chuckles, others with surprise that I'd even have the chutzpah to walk into this house of manly men, many of whom have done their best to put me behind bars and prison walls. Their failure to achieve this wet dream eats at their cops' core, no doubt.

Still, my parrying with the Blue Boys over the years established a certain give-and-take between us, like Officer Dan Bertelli's snide, "Hey, Gold! I got a nice pair of steel cuffs that would go real well with that brown silk suit you're parading around in!"

"Sorry, Bertelli," I shoot back. "I don't wear cheap jewelry." Laughter of the smart-alecky sort follows me upstairs to the detectives' squad room on the second floor.

The air up here stings with cigar and cigarette smoke. The room's noisy with ringing telephones, the complaints of hapless victims, resentful suspects, annoyed ladies of the night hauled in before their nightwork's barely begun, and the whines of other uncooperative characters chafing in handcuffs.

Most of the cops are in shirtsleeves, many sitting at their desks and yammering on their phones. Like the uniformed cops downstairs, these fellas give me suspicious stares, too. I have fun giving them a cheery wave on my way to Adair's office.

After a quick knock on the dirty glass pane of his door, I walk inside. Adair, like the boys in his squad, is also in shirtsleeves. He looks up from his cluttered desk as I walk in, the clumps of files and papers doing only a fair job of hiding years of cigarette burns and coffee stains on the battered desktop. The window behind him might have a swell view of the nighttime city, but the sooty, smeared glass kills it. The peeling green paint on the walls only adds to the general dinginess of the place.

Funny, the city can afford an army of janitors to keep the fancy wood paneling polished in the Mayor's and city councilmen's digs but can't afford a few buckets of paint for a cop's office. Makes me wonder if the city's big shots have the same less-than-friendly attitude about cops as I do.

Adair's not happy to see me. Before I even have a chance to say hello or tell him why I'm here, he snaps, "No. I'm not gonna tell you about that meeting at Mrs. Sheinbaum's house."

"Okay, then I won't ask," I say, and sit down in one of the two wooden chairs opposite his desk. "But tell me why the police are ignoring Nick's killing."

He gives that a dismissive wave, and leans back in his squeaky chair. "What makes you think we're ignoring it?"

"C'mon, Adair. Don't dance around with me. You're a lousy dancer. If the department was really working Nick's case, they'd be all over the crew who worked for Nick. They'd be all over me, too. But nobody's seen so much as a cop car tailing us."

I take out my pack of smokes, light one, and look straight at Adair.

He drums his fingers on his desk, and avoids looking at me.

"All right," I say. "What about just you? Will *you* help me find Nick's killer?"

He picks through the files on his desk, acts like I'm not even there.

I try again. "Then how about this? Will you try to stop me from looking for whoever killed Nick?"

He keeps fiddling with his files, his eyes darting to the door.

I get it. "Listen, Adair," I say, getting up and buttoning my coat, "I'm hungry. How about we grab a bite to eat? My treat."

He stops fidgeting with the files, looks at me, says quietly, "Where?"

"Pete's Luncheonette," I say. "People there mind their own business. It's over on—"

"I know the place. Half an hour," he says, and nods to the door.

I take the hint. On my way out, I open the door wide for effect, say loud enough for the squad room to hear, "Well, thanks for nothing, Lieutenant."

I leave the door open when he shouts, "Get lost, Gold!"

Pete's is humming with the late dinner crowd when I walk in. Several tables and counter seats are already taken. Neighborhood types chatter with friends or have their faces deep in the evening editions of the newspapers, or study the racing forms, or scan the showbiz rags for the casting calls. I hang my coat and cap on the rack by the door and find an empty seat at the counter.

Doris looks me over with the attitude of a mother hen. "You look lousy," she says. "It's not like you to look lousy. Even those scars on your face are drooping. How about a nice steak and a piece of pie to perk you up?"

"Just coffee," I say. "Maybe later on the steak. I'm waiting for someone."

"Someone you're not crazy about?"

"How'd you guess?"

"You have that look in your eyes," she says, pouring me a cup, "like you have heartburn or maybe expecting to have it."

"Hah. You might be right," I say.

"Then you must be waiting for a cop."

I try to laugh it off, but the best I can do is a not-so-innocent chuckle. "Now, why would you say that?"

"Well," she says, looking me over and lifting my chin, "you don't look sad, so you're not in hot water over some dame. And you don't look like you're nursing a headache, which tells me you're not having any trouble you can't handle with the tough crowd you run with. That just leaves a cop. Only a cop would give you heartburn."

"You're too smart for me, Doris."

Every street-savvy year she's lived is in the warmth of her small smile and the wisdom behind her aging eyes. "A good waitress knows how to read her customers, that's all."

"I depend on it. That, and the fact that you make the best coffee in town," I add with a wink. I lean across the counter, say quietly to Doris, "Listen, the cop's name is Adair, Lieutenant Liam Adair. Midtown precinct."

She says just as quietly, "I suppose I should forget the name until I might need to remember it?"

A nod is all I need to give her. She accepts it, and goes along the counter to another customer.

I'm finishing the last of my coffee when Adair walks in. He hangs his coat on the rack but keeps his hat. His badly tailored gray suit is rumpled, a testament to a life of crummy pay by a cop not on the take. He sees me, and cocks his head toward an empty table in the corner. I join him there.

He pushes his hat back on his head, gives me a sour look, then looks down at the table before looking back at me. His face—chunky, muscular, and usually wearing a tough expression—is knotted with doubt. "You know the score, Gold. Helping you would go against every inch of the bond I have with the guys on the force. And besides, I don't like you."

"That doesn't keep me awake nights, lieutenant."

"No, I guess it wouldn't," he says with a chuckle that enjoys itself a bit too much.

"But you're here," I say, "so maybe you like me just a little. Enough, anyway, to help me find Nick's killer."

"Maybe I'm just here to eat dinner," he says. "You did say it's your treat."

There are few things in life more insincere than a cop's smile.

I wave to Doris, signal her to come take our order.

She arrives with her pad and pencil and an attitude of curiosity mixed with caution when she looks at Adair. "What can I get you?" she says. "Special tonight is meatloaf with mushroom gravy. It comes with buttered green beans if you want 'em. A buck-five."

"Sure," Adair says, and adds, "Put it on Gold's tab."

Doris gives me a raised eyebrow. I give her a shrug. "Yeah, my tab."

She returns my shrug, her eyebrow still raised. "You still having that steak? It's two-twenty-five."

"Rare," I say, "and with sliced potatoes on the side."

"That'll cost you thirty-five cents extra. You do like throwing money around, don't you, Cantor," she says and walks away to put in our dinner order.

Adair and I go back to sizing each other up. "Well, lieutenant," I say, "if you're not here to help me find Nick's killer, why are you here?"

He leans back in his chair, drums his fingers on the table, and looks at me like I'm a pest he can't get rid of no matter how many times he's tried. "Because you're a pain in my ass," he says, "and I won't get rid of you until you tell me what you know about Fortunato's death."

"I already told you what I know when I faced that cagey crowd at Mom Sheinbaum's this afternoon. I've got nothing else to say about it."

"Uh-huh," Adair says. I see by his squint and hear in his voice that he doesn't believe me. "So you were on the street when Fortunato hit the pavement. Big deal. What I want to know, Gold, is what you were doing there in the first place."

"And you want to know this, why? You going rogue, lieutenant?" I can't resist giving him a smile so loaded with sarcasm it wouldn't surprise me if Adair spit in my face.

All he gives me is a sneery curl of his fleshy lip. "Never mind about me," he says. "I want to know how you figure into this."

"And I want to know why the cops are tossing Nick's killing into the trash can. Look, I know you, Adair. You don't like unsolved murders. You sniff around for suspects like a rat on the trail of cheese. So tell me why the department is stepping away from this, and maybe, just maybe, I'll let slip something that might interest you."

Adair's sneer turns into the self-satisfied smile of a guy realizing he holds all the cards. It gives me the creeps. "It's not a good idea to hold out on me, Gold," he says. "If you've got information, spill it, or do I have to remind you that withholding evidence is a felony in this state. It can get you up to four years behind bars. And let's face it, you wouldn't like prison. The food's lousy, and they won't let you wear those fancy suits."

"Oh, I don't know," I say. "Life can get pretty cozy in a prison cell, especially if my cellmate has talented hands, among her other criminally delightful attributes."

He doesn't enjoy the joke.

"Listen, Adair," I say, "I don't give a fig for your laws, and you know it. And you know why. So if the day ever comes when Johnny Law decides I'm a human being and won't put me in jail for holding hands with a woman, maybe then I'll take your laws a little more seriously. In the meantime—"

"Here's your steak, Cantor." It's Doris with my platter. She puts it on the table, puts Adair's platter down, too, and slides me the check. Adair digs into his meatloaf with the gusto of a guy who knows he's not paying for it. I cut into my steak, let the juice run into the potatoes before I scoop up a forkful. The pleasure of the tasty spuds followed by bites of succulent steak fortifies me enough to ask a dangerous question: "Did Sig Loreale put the kibosh on the police looking into Nick's killing?"

Adair keeps eating, doesn't look up from his meatloaf and green beans.

I try again. "Look, Adair, I know you're one of the few cops not in Sig's pocket, but you still know what goes on. If Sig's behind the squelch, and if you know why, you can tell me. Sure, we don't like each other; I don't like how you make your dough, you don't like how I make mine and how I live my life. But we've always played the game square with each other. So whatever you tell me will stay with me. Neither Sig nor your cop buddies will ever know."

He stops chewing, looks at me like he wants to laugh, which he does after he swallows. The laugh's a short one, just enough to needle me. "You don't get it, do you, Gold. I'm not here to make deals with you."

"Then why are you here, Adair? And don't tell me it's for the free dinner, or just to find out what I know about Nick. You didn't even look at me when I mentioned Sig's name. Why? Afraid something in your face would give the game away? Are you afraid Sig would send his thugs after you? Are you afraid of Sig?"

Adair's muscular face goes hard as a pile of rocks. "No, I am not afraid of Sig Loreale. I'm not afraid of him, his thugs, or any of the gangsters he surrounds himself with. And that includes you."

"But you're afraid of something," I say, pushing back. "You're afraid of not knowing what's going on. It grates against your cop's soul. It grates against mine, too, Adair. So let's help each other. Let's find out why Nick was killed and who did it." I stuff another piece of steak into my mouth. It doesn't taste so good anymore.

"Why?" Adair says. "So you can exact revenge? Your kind of justice is no better than murder."

"What if I promise to let you have him?"

"Or her," he says with a sarcastic snort.

My nod hides my choke on the idea. Instead, I say, "But I can't give you the killer, can I, Adair. The department doesn't want the killer found. The department wants the whole thing to go away. Whose path would get cleared, Adair?"

Our chit-chat is interrupted by a strange, short, skinny guy who's suddenly standing at our table. The guy's wearing a dilapidated tweed coat and a sweat-stained fedora, his eyes crinkled with hard living, his hands in his coat pockets, a two-day stubble darkening his hollow cheeks. He says in a wheezy growl, "You're Cantor Gold, right? You gotta come with me. You too," he says to Adair. The guy's tobacco breath could shrivel every tree in Central Park. Adair looks the guy up and down as if he's a fly he wants to swat away. The nose of a gun sliding from the guy's coat pocket changes Adair's mind.

I thought I knew just about every hoodlum, con artist, or desperado working my side of the street, but this guy's a blank. I say, "Who the hell are you, and why should we follow you anywhere?"

"It doesn't matter who I am," he wheezes, "but unless you want me to shoot this place up, you'll come along with me. Quietly."

The look in his eyes, mean, bitter, convinces me he'd do it and not care who got in the way of his bullets. He'd probably even it enjoy it.

Adair looks at me. I look at Adair. Our silent conversation decides that, yeah, the two of us could take the guy down, but the chances are good he'd get off a few shots and bloody or kill some of the customers eating dinner at their tables.

Adair says, "Okay, buddy, we'll go with you. Just take it easy. No one has to get hurt."

The guy gives me a warning side-eye as I reach inside my jacket pocket. "Just getting my wallet," I say. "Gotta pay the tab. You wouldn't want me to stiff the waitress, would you?"

He says, "If anything besides your hand and your wallet comes outta that jacket, you and a lotta people in here are gonna get dead."

I pull my wallet out slowly, open it, take out a fiver for the three-buck, sixty-five cent tab and put it on the table. Doris will pocket the rest.

The guy with the gun in his pocket gets behind us when Adair and I walk to the door. A few neighbors at tables and the counter give me a nod and a wave. I nod back, keeping things as normal as I can. I don't want to give the lunatic behind us any reason to shoot the place up.

Adair and I take our coats from the rack, slip them on, and head out to the street. A blue-and-white Chevy is idling at the curb, its chrome bumper catching the light of a streetlamp. I can't see the driver, just his hand out the driver's window with a twenty-dollar bill our captor grabs.

The back door opens. The guy with the gun pushes us inside. He slams the door shut, then gets lost among the crowds on the street.

There's someone else in the back seat, someone I can't see but I feel something hard crash down on my head. And then I barely see a thing, barely hear Adair's grunt, barely feel the car speed away, and now I see, hear, and feel nothing.

Chapter Fifteen

I wake up a little. I don't know how long I've been out or where we are but the car rolls to a stop. Wherever we are has the throat-gagging stench of a swamp.

My head hurts. So do my wrists and my arm sockets. As my head clears, I realize my hands are tied behind my back, pulling hard on my arms.

I hear a groan next to me. It's Adair. He's waking up, too. I assume his arms are trussed up like mine.

The car doors open on either side of us. Two guys, likely the driver and the guy in the backseat who knocked us out, pull us out of the car.

Our feet squish in mud, our legs tangle in reeds. If this swamp, wherever it is, is anything like the swamps around New York Bay, the reeds are thick with deadly copperhead snakes and other critters I'd rather not have feast on my ankles.

In the clouded moonlight, I barely see our captor's faces, and with their fedoras pulled low all I see are their mouths and chins anyway. The guy holding me is a little shorter than the guy holding Adair, but not by much. Both guys are wearing rubber boots. I guess they knew they'd be taking us to this muddy killing ground. That's what it is, a killing ground.

The shorter guy, who appears to be in charge, says to the taller, "Get in the car. Keep the engine running."

The driver does as he's told.

That leaves Adair without a captor, but there's nothing he can do to escape since the guy holding me has just cocked his gun. It's the hammer of a revolver, a big one.

He throws me down to the ground, into water thick with mud. I get a mouthful of the nasty stuff. It stifles my groan.

I can't decide whether to try to get up and die with dignity when the bullet will certainly come, or just lie here and wait for a copperhead to slither up from the reeds, shoot me full of its deadly venom and slowly eat me. I might be too weak and trussed up to accomplish the first, but I'm too damned angry to wait around for the second. I might as well die with some fight in me.

With a groan, I push my knees into the mud, try to push myself up from the reeds. I hear the crack of gunfire.

Adair. The shooter must've killed Adair first.

I'm just about upright when something slams into me, nearly sending me crashing down into the mud again.

"Dammit!" I hear Adair holler. "I tried to push him down, not crash into you."

I manage to get a little traction and stay upright. The gunman Adair pushed is now down in the mud.

Anger runs through me like a burning rod of vengeance. Anger at letting some creep get the better of me. Anger at not knowing what the hell's been going on since last night. I stomp my foot in the guy's ribs and chest. Once, twice, three, four, five times, until I hear Adair yell, "Let it go, Gold! You're killing him!"

There's another crack of gunfire, this time from the guy who was sent to the car. He's running out now, sloshing through the mud and reeds toward Adair.

I slam into him, knock the aim of his second shot, sending it wild. Adair joins me. With our hands tied behind us, we're two muddy bulls headbutting the guy: my head in his gut, Adair's in his face. When the guy falls down, screaming, it's Adair now whose deadly anger takes over. He kicks the guy senseless, and then some.

I have to pull him off. When he finally stops, all we hear now is the gentle lapping of muddy pools of water.

Adair turns his back to me. "Untie me," he says.

When we're back to back, I can feel his arms and his whole body shaking. I clumsily fiddle with the knot on his wrists until I finally set him free.

His fingers still shaking, he unties my hands.

We both scramble for the two killers' guns, and take their wallets from their pockets. We're not interested in any cash, just finding out who the hell they are.

The shorter guy's driver's license says he's Willam L. Stang, from Albany. The taller guy is also from Albany. According to his driver's license, his name's Michael Colnick.

Adair says, "Out-of-town killers. Recognize either of their names?"

I shake my head no. "I'm more interested in knowing who sent them. And why."

"I'll see what the department has on them," Adair says. "Maybe they're in our files. I'll check with the Albany cops, too, see if they can trace who might've contracted them." He nods at the wallets, licenses, and guns we're still holding. "We'd better get rid of these," he says. We toss the wallets and licenses far into the water, then break the guns down and throw the parts into the swamp in different directions.

"That's what they had in mind for us," I say. "Toss us into the swamp and let us sink, never to be found. At least not until the fish nibbled us down to the bone. They never even bothered to take my gun." I pull the muddy .38 from its holster, slide it back again.

"Mine either," Adair says, checking his own. "They didn't have to."

"Come on, let's get outta here," I say.

But Adair doesn't move. He just sighs a deep, tight, miserable sigh. "We just killed two guys, Gold," he says. He sounds like his own life just ended.

I wonder if this is Adair's first kill. He's not a trigger happy cop, at least as far as I know. I hope I never get the chance to find out. But his bulgy, bulldog face sure as hell looks miserable.

Then his eyes widen for a second, as if an idea clicks in his brain. "We'll wipe down the Chevy, inside and out, even the door handles. Everything."

"Like we were never here," I say.

"Like nobody was ever here."

This is a different Adair, all right, than the one I thought I knew, the honest cop doing his best to keep his nose clean in a dirty system. That Adair would never hide two killings.

Then again, I'm not about to tell him how to survive in that dirty system. I just follow him to the Chevy.

We use our wet handkerchiefs to wipe every surface of the car. When we're done, I use my handkerchief to open the glove compartment, take the car's registration and other papers out. The registration's a phony, in the name of John Smith of Haverstraw, New York.

Adair says, "Smart move."

"Glad you appreciate my criminal instincts," I say.

He gives that a snort, as close to a laugh as he'll allow himself. "Let's get the license plates."

"With what?" I say. "You carry screwdrivers in your pockets?"

"Check the trunk. Maybe there's tools or something in there we can use."

There's no screwdriver in the trunk, but there's a satchel with tools for changing tires: a jack, a tire iron, and a heavy steel prybar. The prybar does the job nicely.

We toss the prybar, license plates, and the papers from the glove compartment into the swamp, and watch the plates and prybar sink, the papers soak and shred.

I say, "My criminal instincts tell me there's one more job to do."

Even in the clouded moonlight, I can see Adair's muddied face take on a sickly look, as if something bitter is lodged deep in his throat.

"Take a walk, lieutenant," I say.

He doesn't move. He says nothing. Just stares at me with that sickly look.

"Go on. Walk. I'll catch up to you," I say.

He finally turns, starts to walk away. "No," he says over his shoulder, "that's not a good idea."

He's right. I don't know where the hell we are, but we'd better not be seen together when we make our way back to the city. It would be bad for him. It would be worse for me. He knows it would be worse for me. And I know the only reason he's letting me get away with a killing is because he killed a guy, too. That's what's bitter in the back of his cop's throat.

I give him a few minutes to get far enough away for me to get to work.

I open the Chevy's hood, pull out small but heavy parts of the engine. The water will destroy any fingerprints but I wipe everything down anyway, take no chances that something doesn't sink. Then I put the car in neutral and roll it to the water. The mud and reeds fight me, but I keep pushing until the car's own motion completes the job and the swamp swallows it.

I put the engine parts into the two dead guys' coat pockets.

I'm soaking wet with swamp water and sweat on this chilly November night, especially after I push the dead weight of each guy into the water, the heavy engine parts sinking them deep into the reedy swamp. The copperheads will have a feast.

I scoop up handfuls of muddy water, do the best I can to wash the mud from my face. It's an odd moment to find something funny, considering I was almost killed and killed a guy myself, but I laugh a little at the idea that if people recoil from me on the street when they see a female in men's duds, they'll likely faint at the sight of the muddy monster emerging from the swamp.

After a soaked slosh through the mud and reeds, I come out at a tree-lined road. There's nothing but an Esso gas station and a sign identifying the place as MOE'S GAS & OIL – BEST SERVICE ON STATEN ISLAND.

At least I'm still in the City of New York, though I'm closer to New Jersey than Times Square.

The gas station's closed for the night, which is probably just as well; seeing the state of me, Moe would likely call the cops.

There's a phone booth next to the door, though.

I call Judson. I don't see an address for the gas station or road sign on the street, so I give him the name of the gas station. He says he'll find it.

It'll take him at least an hour to drive from his place in Manhattan, cross the bay on the ferry, and drive to this empty outback on Staten Island.

Shivering, cold to the marrow, I settle in to wait. I wish I had a drink to warm me. I wish I had a smoke to calm me, but my pack of Chesterfields and my lighter are gone, probably fell out of my pocket when I struggled in the swamp. All I have are my thoughts, none of which are warm or comforting. The worst is the thought that I killed, that my anger, an anger that always rumbles deep inside me, an anger I've earned but I keep in check, exploded into an act of death. Somehow I have to find a way to live with that. I have to, or it could eat me alive.

Judson finally arrives. During the ride back to town, I ask

him to look into who owns the building where Abby wants to open her fancy club and bookie joint, and to find out all he can about William L. Stang and Michael Colnick, hired guns from Albany. Sure, Adair might have information about those two in police files, or can get records from his cop colleagues upstate, but Judson has his own sources. Deeper ones. Much deeper.

Chapter Sixteen

A shower helps. The tumbler of scotch I brought with me helps more. The hot needles of water ease the knots in my muscles. The whiskey eases the anger that led me to kill.

I don't like killing. Just like Nick mattered to me and mattered to the crew who worked for him, or the thug who muscled Nick probably mattered to someone, William L. Stang and Michael Colnick might've mattered to someone, too, even if it was only their mothers.

But I don't like being targeted, either, and I certainly wouldn't like being shot to death and buried in a swamp, which is what Stang and Colnick were clearly hired to do. It was them or me, or Adair.

That's the story I decide I can live with, especially after I step out of the shower and pour another scotch. Soon, though, after a couple of hefty swallows, I realize I could tell myself that story all night long but it still wouldn't ease the rotten feeling of having taken a life—two lives, if you count the guy Adair killed but I dumped into the swamp. Whoever came up with that saying *in vino veritas*—in wine there's truth—really knew what they were talking about.

There's been too much death these last two days. First Nick, then the thug in Nick's apartment, now the two guys in the swamp. I feel like I should exchange my bathrobe for a shroud.

But better a shroud than handcuffs.

I don't bother to turn the lights on in my living room, just sink into my favorite chair, let the neighborhood's neon lights flow through my window, let their colors wash over the white terrycloth of my bathrobe and lull me into the illusion that life is still beautiful.

The ringing phone pierces that reverie.

At first I try to ignore it, hope the caller would finally give up.

Then I think it might be Judson with information about Stang and Colnick. I'd figured he'd look into it tomorrow morning after a night's sleep, but maybe the idea of letting the assignment just dangle out there gave him an itch he absolutely has to scratch, even at nearly midnight.

The voice after my "Hello," isn't Judson's. It's silkier. It's Lily's voice.

"Cantor? I've been trying to reach you for hours. I even went to the Green Door Club, but Peg said you hadn't been in. Look, I know it's late, but I have to see you. Would you like to come to my hotel? Or I can come to your place, if you'd prefer."

After the events of the last two days and the ordeal tonight, what I really need is sleep. What I don't need is the company of the woman whose secret goings-on could strangle me.

What I really want is Lily. "Come to my place. The address is—"

"I know."

Of course she does.

She's at my door less than a half hour later. She's in her white cashmere coat, which opens to a sleek velvet dress, its color a deep burgundy, like wine.

I'm still in my terry robe.

I'm about to ask her what's so important that she has to see me in the middle of the night, but I don't get the chance. As soon as she steps inside, she's against me, her arms around my neck, her lips on mine.

Her kiss washes away the taste of death from my mouth. Her body against me gives me a soft, warm jolt of life. My fingers run through her hair, those elegant short blond windblown strands, the shimmering crown of the naughty princess who's in a hurry to live.

She pulls away from our kiss. "I had to see you, Cantor," she says, her gray eyes only half open but full of feeling. "I've been worried about you all day. The way you left Mrs. Sheinbaum's place today, with Lieutenant Adair escorting you out, was painful to watch. The idea of the famous Cantor Gold given the shove by the police—why are you laughing?"

"I've never heard myself described as famous. Famous for what?"

"Oh, for a lot of things." She slides away from me, takes her coat off and hands it to me to hang up in the hall closet, which I dutifully do. "You're famous for things like slipping through whatever nets the police have tried to tangle you in," she says. "Things like living your own way, even risking your life to do it. Oh, you are very famous, indeed, Cantor Gold."

"Uh-huh," I say dully, and follow her into the living room, where I turn on a lamp. Its light shines on her hair, her velvet dress. "None of that answers the question of why you want to see me in the middle of the night."

She turns to look at me, puzzlement in her eyes. "I told you. I'm worried about you. I want to make sure you're all right."

"I'm fine," I say.

"No, you're not. What I see is someone who's exhausted. What I felt when I held you was a body tight with—well, I don't know what with, but whatever it is, I think it frightens you."

She's hit the target, a target I'd rather she didn't see so clearly. "We all live with a little fear," I say, making light of it. "A dose of fear is one of the tools which keeps people like us alive, or at least keeps us on our toes to outsmart the cops. Oh, but you don't have to do that anymore, do you, Lily. You don't have to outsmart the cops. You're the most protected lawbreaker I know. That's what *you're* famous for. And now you even have the protection of Sig Loreale, or at least you're in cahoots with him. He's the most dangerous guy I know. Whatever it is you're doing with him, remember this: whatever he's in the game for, if anything or anyone gets in his way, he won't care how much the local cops or the Feds give you a pass. He'll snuff you out like a cigar stub."

"I can take care of myself," she says. The confidence in her voice is betrayed by the slight shiver of her body. She hides it quickly. Like me, she understands that feeling fear is one thing; showing it can be a dangerous mistake.

She sits down on the couch; reclines is more like it, one arm on the armrest, her legs to the side. Her burgundy velvet dress ripples and shimmers in the lamplight like a river of wine tempting me to dive in and drink.

"And anyway," she says, breaking into my carnal imaginings, "Loreale likes you, Cantor."

"I doubt it," I say, after a snort of a laugh. "Friendship isn't one of his strong points."

"But it's true. I can hear it when he speaks of you."

I answer that with a curt, "Hm." I don't know if the idea of Sig liking me, or even caring about me one way or the other, pleases me or scares me to death. More likely the latter. "How about a drink?" I say.

"Whatever you're having."

I pour her a tumbler scotch, another for myself, and sit down facing her on the other end of the couch.

We sip our drinks, staring at each other over the rims of our glasses. I do my best to probe her eyes, discover what that smoky gray hides. She doesn't shrink from my gaze. She matches it. She's every bit my equal, and I'm a sucker for it, a sucker for her, which means I have to guard against it, guard against the woman who's brought her danger and her secrets crashing into my life. "Why are you really here, Lily?"

"Cantor, for god's sake," she says, sitting up and putting her drink on the side table before she slides toward me. "How many times do I have to tell you? I had to see you, make sure you're all right." The way she traces my scars with her fingertip brings back those carnal dreams.

It's an effort to take her hand away, to stop my craving for her from overtaking me, but I do it. "I want to believe you," I say. "I really do. But you bring too many secrets with you, Lily, secrets that aren't just yours anymore, but secrets that tangle me up now, too. You bring them along with whatever's going on between you and Sig and Mom Sheinbaum and Lieutenant Adair. Those people have been in my life a long time, Lily, especially Sig and Mom, and suddenly they want me quiet and out of their way. They want me out of your way, too, to do whatever it is they want you to do. If you want me to believe you give a damn about me—"

"I do! I give more than just a damn, Cantor."

"All right, then tell me what the hell is going on," I say with the angry force of a bark. "Why is Nick Fortunato's murder an inconvenience? What's it got to do with whatever business you and your new friends are cooking up? Get rid of the secrets, Lily. If you keep those secrets, you can't have me, and that would—"

She eats the rest of my words with her lips on mine. There's a hunger in her kiss, a craving as emotional as it is lustful. I've felt the inescapable power of that craving only once before, from the woman I loved and lost years ago and whose death still haunts me. But here's that hunger again, that demand of me again, that breathtaking, terrifying possibility of love again.

We are two wild animals, primitive in our needs, selfish in satisfying them.

We are tender lovers, soothing each other's battered hearts and damaged souls.

We are two outlaws in the safe haven of night.

I hear, "Cantor," whispered into my sleepy haze, feel warm fingers slide across my lips.

My eyes open a little. In the darkness of my bedroom, with only the light of streetlamps and nightspot marquees floating through the window, I see Lily's face bathed in neon colors.

"Cantor," she says again, my name riding on her breath like silk floating in the air, "you know, I don't have to live in Chicago. I could live here, in New York."

My eyes are fully open now. I take her fingers from my lips, see Lily through the neon glow. "What are you saying?"

"You know what I'm saying. I'd rather be near you than far away from you. I've fallen for you, Cantor."

Pleasure and alarm rise up and battle within me. "That's a little sudden, isn't it? We met only last night."

She strokes my lips again, then slides her fingers along my cheek. "Sometimes you just know." Neon light ripples along her face as she speaks. The effect is beautiful as a shimmering rainbow, and frightening as a carnival funhouse. "Sometimes you just know when it's right," she says. "I knew it the minute you walked into the Green Door Club. You stopped my heart, Cantor."

The way I knew that Sophie stopped my heart.

"Cantor? What's wrong? I just felt your body tense up. What are you thinking about? Or no, no, that's not it. *Who* are you thinking about?"

My gut's gone tight as a fist, a fist that holds memories I've kept locked up so they wouldn't burn me to ash. But now Lily Vardanian, beautiful, smart, dangerous, and with secrets of her own, is prying that fist open. "All right," I say, sitting up. "There was someone, a woman I loved and lost. I'll tell you about her, but it comes with a price. A price you have to be willing to pay if we stand any chance together."

As she sits up next to me, the colored light brushes her gleaming blond hair then slides away, leaving us both in darkness. "If your price is me telling you about my arrangement with Loreale and the others, you're asking too much. You know how the game is played, Cantor. There are deals you just can't break, not if you want to survive."

"Are you telling me your life is in danger?"

"Isn't it always?" she says with a laugh. "It's the world we both live in. Even with all those protections you think I have, if I make even one slip, or put the wrong word into the wrong ears, those protections go down the drain. I'd end up either in handcuffs or dead. Even being here with you is dangerous for me. So please, Cantor, ask me anything else, but don't ask me about the job I've been hired to do."

She can't pay the price I need paid, and I'm not willing to pay the price of ignoring her secrets.

I slide away from her a little, my fist of memories closing tight, locking the memories away again. "Can you at least tell me why they want Nick's murder shoved under the rug?"

After a sigh loaded with as much sadness as annoyance, she says, "It has nothing to do with Fortunato being murdered. Well, not the fact of it, anyway." There's a slight edge to her voice. I guess she didn't like me moving away from her. "It has to do with you."

"Me?"

She takes my chin in her hand and turns my face to hers. "Listen to me, Cantor. If you weren't Fortunato's friend they'd ignore his killing and let the police handle it in their usual way, no doubt with Loreale behind the scenes to make sure they found the killer. After all, Loreale was business partners with Fortunato, and it's likely he'd want to know who's behind the hit."

Sure. There's no way Sig would let the murder of one of his associates just slide, even though he wants me to steer clear of it.

Lily has more to say, her voice quiet but insistent now. "Loreale knew that Fortunato was killed on his birthday. He also knew that you'd be at Fortunato's apartment to celebrate. Knowing how tight you were with the guy, Loreale figured you wouldn't let the killing go, that you'd get involved, and that you'd snoop in every direction. Loreale figured that sooner or later you'd bump into our business, which is exactly what you did when you showed up at Mrs. Sheinbaum's today."

I take a cigarette from the pack I keep on my bedside table. I reach for my lighter, then remember that the lighter never made it back to my apartment. It's now at the bottom of the swamp, where the two guys I pushed into the muck will have no use for it, or my pack of Chesterfields that's down there, too. They won't have the pleasure of a smoke anymore, but I will.

I find a book of matches in the drawer, and as I light my smoke and draw that first, satisfying inhale, the match flame shines its hard light on Lily. It makes me wonder how many other secrets she's keeping, like if she knows about the thugs sent to kill me and Adair tonight. But that's a question I won't ask. If she knows, she won't tell. It will be just another of her secrets. If she doesn't know, mentioning it would be a lousy idea.

Instead, I ask, "Lily, did Sig ever mention anyone named Abby?"

"No, why? Is she the woman you loved?"

The idea makes me laugh, a short sharp laugh more acid than sweet. "No," I say. "Just curious."

She takes my cigarette from my hand, takes a deep drag, then gives it back to me. Her exhaled smoke drifts into a sliver of neon light. So does her cheek as she leans toward me. "Cantor, you need to be careful. I don't know who this Abby person is or what she has to do with Loreale or your friend Nick, but I can tell you no one by that name is part of our plans." She leans closer to me, kisses my cheek, slides her cheek against mine. "Please, Cantor, don't toss me away."

Every part of me wants to hold her, touch her, taste her, love her, but it's that last bit that tangles me up. "Then tell me what I need to know, tell me what's going on with you and that gang at Mom Sheinbaum's place so I can find my way through this mess and stay alive while I search for Nick's killer. Bring me inside your life, Lily."

"I—can't," she says.

A warm tear seeps from her cheek to mine.

I separate us and turn on the bedside lamp. "Then I can't trust you, Lily."

It twists me up to see her wipe the tear from her cheek, and gives me the shivers when she strokes my face, her fingertip lingering along the little knife-shaped scar above my lip.

I take her hand away.

She clears her throat to get rid of a sob. "Maybe it's better that I go."

"Yeah, sure, maybe it is." It comes out chillier than I want.

She climbs out of bed, gathers her clothes, but before she leaves the bedroom, she says, "This woman you loved and lost, you're talking about someone dead, aren't you."

I don't answer her.

"I pity you, Cantor. You're in love with a memory."

Chapter Seventeen

I'm counting on a morning jolt of Doris's strong coffee to clear my head of the tangled schemes of people I thought I knew, loosen the grip of death that's threatened to choke me since Nick's murder, and knock my heart back into place after last night's plunge from ecstasy with Lily to distrust and heartbreak.

Dressing well has always helped me keep a solid sense of myself, but my fingers are still slow and sleepy this morning as I finish buttoning my pale peach shirt, tie my light blue tie, slip my .38 into my shoulder rig, and put on the jacket of my navy blue suit. I'm just about to collect my coat and cap from the hall closet and head out to Pete's Luncheonette for Doris's good coffee and a bit of breakfast when there's a buzz at my apartment door. When I open it, Chickie D'Andrea, whose baggy brown overcoat and crummy fedora are insults to the tailoring and hat-making professions, stands in my doorway. "Hello, Cantor," he says, his foggy voice more annoying than soothing this morning. Worse, he's grinning at me like we're the best of friends. When he opens his coat and takes his hat off, his gray suit gives him all the panache of wet cardboard, his yellow shirt has a grease stain his black tie can't quite hide, and his mousey brown crew cut makes his face look even chubbier than usual.

He walks into my apartment without being asked. "Yeah, yeah, I know, you're surprised to see me," he says on his way to my living room. "Didn't I say yesterday that I want to help you?"

"Help me? That sure wasn't the impression I got when you pulled a gun on me at Abby's place after she drugged me. And you were anything but friendly when you were the guy holding Abby's skirts at that big new joint of hers."

He answers with a *tsk* and a dismissive wave. Smiling a smile that makes him look like a scheming chipmunk, he says, "Don't believe everything you see, Cantor. I can pull off an act when it suits my purpose."

"Is that so? If that sniveling creature I saw yesterday was all an act, you should go on the stage."

"I was!" he says, laughing. "Oh, nothing big-time like the Broadway types in your neighborhood. I had my fun in the last days of vaudeville before it all folded. I did all kinds of schtick; y'know, taking pratfalls, hamming it up in crazy costumes. Mostly I was what they used to call a baggy-pants comic."

I find the comic part tough to buy, but in that coat and shlumpy gray suit I can buy the baggy pants bit. "Must've been tough to give up the spotlight," I say, doing my best not to laugh at the guy.

"I still keep my hand in now and then," he says. "Kids parties, lodge conventions, that sorta thing, make a coupla bucks here and there just for fun. But I can tell you, I make a lot more dough in the betting racket than I ever did in show biz." He may be happy about the money, but I'm pretty sure I hear a note of nostalgia in his voice. He gets past it, though. "Listen, Cantor, I wasn't kidding yesterday when I said I want to help you. And I'm in a position to do it. I was on the inside of Nick's business, and now I'll be on the inside of Abby's operation."

"Uh-huh, so what? So will Mike, maybe Freddie, too," I say, "but they're not rushing to put their lives on the line to help me find Nick's killer. What makes you so brave?"

"Loyalty." The guy says it like he's a good citizen about to recite the Pledge of Allegiance, or maybe cry. "Loyalty, because Nick trusted me to handle the numbers, and you know that numbers are everything in making book. Bad numbers can kill the day's cash haul. When the odds sheets came in, Nick knew I'd go over them like a dog sniffing for meat. He never second-guessed me. Great guy to work for."

"What about Abby? She has a knack for numbers, too, and Nick put her in charge of the day-to-day running of the joint. Did she ever look over your shoulder to check your sheets?"

"Sure, once in a while," he says with a shrug that's probably less easygoing than he'd like it to be. "It was part of her job, I guess, being the manager and all. I didn't hold it against her. But I gotta tell you, Cantor, I wasn't crazy about how she treated Nick. Always pushing him to make the operation bigger. She never knew when to keep her mouth shut, if you ask me." He sits down on the couch, where just last night Lily reclined like a delicious diva. Chickie's heavy sit-down is more like a floundering whale.

I stand over him. "So why didn't Nick fire her?"

"You know how Nick was," he says, fingering his hat, "not an angry bone in his body. Abby's carping was just water off a duck's back to him. As long as Abby did her job as good as she did, he overlooked how pushy she could be. A lot of the crew, though—well, we couldn't overlook it. But what could we do? It was Nick's dough that paid us, and Nick thought Abby was swell, so we kept our mouths shut."

A lot of this fits with what Mike said about walking into the office and seeing Abby argue with Nick about just that: expanding the operation. But there's something in Chickie's story that sticks in my craw: maybe Chickie and the other guys didn't like a woman having big ideas and a savvy head for business. Maybe Nick began to sense the rumblings among the crew. And maybe Abby knew it.

"All right, Chickie," I say. "You want to help me? Okay, feed me the dope on what goes on with Abby and her new operation, especially where she's getting the set-up money."

He gives me that scheming chipmunk smile again. It's Chickie's equivalent of stretching his palm out.

I get the point. "Okay, sure, Chickie, I'll make it worth your while."

His smile tightens, becomes a rictus of greed.

I get the point again. I take out my wallet, peel out two twenties and a sawbuck.

"After all," he says, taking the fifty in bills, "like you said, I'm the only one of the crew risking my life."

"True," I admit. "So be careful. If Abby catches on, she might feed you to the wolves."

Two cups of Doris's coffee and a quick breakfast of eggs on a bagel and I'm fortified enough to handle the day. First stop, my office. Even with all the running around since Nick's death, I still have a business to run, clients to satisfy.

I decide to walk there, let this sunny autumn morning clear my head even more. Today's one of those days when New York is at its best, when the textures of the city, the gritty and the glamorous, show up crisp and clear in the crystal sunlight. Colors are brighter. Brick buildings are redder. The gray sidewalks are whiter. Women's coats and hats breeze by me in a glowing swirl of fashionable colors, and men wear their fedoras at more rakish angles. It's enough to lift my spirits, even just a little, take the edge off the gloom of the last couple of death-laden days. By the time I walk through the alleys to the door of my office I'm actually whistling. It's a tune I heard on the jukebox at the Green Door Club the night I met Lily, a catchy new rock-'n'-roll number sung by a couple of teenage guys telling some girl named Little Susie to wake up.

Judson hands me a few messages when I walk in: a society matron on Fifth Avenue, whose tastes run to the more morbid aspects of Medieval iconography, would like me to "obtain" a crucifix she saw in a cathedral on her recent vacation in Spain; a curator at the city's largest museum—a woman who's been tempting me and teasing me for years—wants to have one of our quiet talks about acquiring a little something she's not at liberty to identify just yet; and a guy who can't spend his new money fast enough in his quest for Old Money's nod of respect is desperate for anything French Rococo.

The most interesting messages Judson gives me, though, are what he found out about Stang and Colnick, and who owns the building where Abby's setting up her new operation.

No surprise that Stang and Colnick have arrest records as long as a cross-country railroad, but neither of them have ever served in prison. That's the way it goes a lot of times; well-connected thugs have privileges.

Judson says, "But I haven't been able to trace who hired them for the Staten Island job. I'll keep digging. Meantime, I found out who holds the paper for the building you're interested in. Some outfit called Cosmopolitan Realty Holdings. They're not registered in New York, though. They're a foreign outfit, registered offshore, in the Bahamas. I can't get a line on who they are, haven't been able to dig out the names of the people who actually own the company. Whoever they are, their names are buried deep as a bottomless paper pit. Sound familiar?" he adds, grinning, his eyes boyishly sly slits behind his wire-rims.

I return his grin. It's the same story with this place. My lawyer buried my name so deep in the ownership and tax papers, it would take a team of archaeologists years to excavate the overlapping layers and they'd still never find my name.

Judson says, "Any ideas?" in a tone that says we're both thinking the same thing.

"Uh-huh. I'll see you later."

Judson calls out to me on my way to the door, "Hey! What about these messages from clients?"

"Tell Mrs. Fifth Avenue a trip to Spain is going to cost her. I'll call Miss Tease at the museum another time. And pull that Fragonard we've got stashed down in the vault for Mr. Rococo." I hear Judson chuckling as I go out.

Bensonhurst Benny is in the doorway to Sig's apartment when I get off the elevator. There's no getting past his gorilla-bulk without handing over my .38 and proving I don't have a spare gun or a shiv hidden in my sock. Satisfied that I'm not planning to kill his boss, he says, "He's on the terrace. It's a nice sunny day. Mr. Loreale likes sunny days."

With that cheery if somewhat hard to believe thought, I make my way through the living room, that chamber of memories, and emerge on the terrace that surrounds Sig's penthouse. Sunlight shines on the gold spires and arches that crown the terrace and the building, a lordly introduction to the view of the city that proclaims Sig's power.

Skyscrapers rise to the right and left of me. The elegant serenity of Bryant Park is twenty-three stories below me across the street, with the Beaux-Arts main building of the New York Public Library at its Fifth Avenue head.

Sig, stern and boulder-like in his black overcoat and black homburg, stands in a corner leaning against the terrace wall, his elbows on the ledge. He's smoking a cigar as he looks out on the city whose pockets he picks every minute of every day.

As I approach, he takes his cigar from his mouth, his fleshy lips wet from the cigar's wet end. "What's on your mind now, Cantor?" he says in that slow, gravel-voiced way of his that's been giving me the creeps since I was a kid.

"What do you know about a building owned by an outfit called Cosmopolitan Realty Holdings?" I say.

He takes another puff of his cigar. The smoke gathers under the brim of his homburg, briefly obscuring his eyes. When the smoke clears, I see he's frowning in thought, taking his time thinking about whatever it is he's thinking about.

Finally, after what feels like a lifetime of perpetual night, he says, "Cosmopolitan Realty Holdings. I've never heard of them."

"So you don't have any money tied up with them?"

"No. I do not. What is this about, Cantor?"

"It seems they own a building over on East Fifty-first Street."

He hasn't looked at me even once since I arrived. He just looks out over the city while he smokes his cigar, flicking ash over the ledge. "What does that building have to do with me?"

"You tell me, Sig," I say. "It might have something to do with whatever plans you have with Abby O'Neill."

After another puff of his cigar, its tip glowing red as a warning beacon, he says, "My plans with Miss O'Neill are not your concern."

"Just like your plans with the crowd at the party I crashed at Mom Sheinbaum's place are none of my concern?"

He finally turns to look at me. The heavy lids of his eyes, always at half mast, are even lower now, giving him the appearance of a tough professor about to scold his most obstinate student. "Once again, Cantor, you are involving yourself where you should not. I have told you more than once to stay out of that business."

"What about the business of Nick's murder? Why don't you want it solved, Sig? Do you want me to lay off so badly that you'd even see me dead?"

"I have no wish to see you dead," he says, shrugging as if annoyed by the question. "I have no wish for any harm to come to you at all. Have you been threatened?"

I give that a bitter snort of a laugh. "Is that what they're calling a trip to the Staten Island swamps at gunpoint this season? Listen, Sig, you ever hear of a couple of hired guns out of Albany named Stang and Colnick?"

"I do not recognize either of those names," he says. His jaw tightening, his jowls stiffening, he adds, "Perhaps I should have them brought to me."

"Don't bother. They won't have anything to say."

He understands, doesn't pursue the matter any further, just smiles a tiny, cold smile at the corner of his mouth, and takes a leisurely puff of his cigar. He looks out over the city again. "Is there something I should know about this building on Fifty-first Street?"

"How much do you trust Abby, Sig?"

He takes a deep breath, spreads one arm out like a tour guide showing a view. "You know, Cantor," he says, "it is quite remarkable how clear everything in the city appears on sunny days. When I look down to the street, I can see every person walking along, even from way up here. I can see their hats, their coats. I can see them scurry like ants as they hurry along. And when I look out and across the city, every building is clear, every line and window is crisp in the sunshine. However, I do not see why a building on East Fifty-first Street should stand out among these thousands of others, but apparently you do, Cantor, and apparently Miss O'Neill has something to do with it."

I take out a cigarette and a matchbook from my inside jacket pocket, light a smoke, lean against the terrace wall, and take my time doing my own thinking. It could be Sig is playing me, playing ignorant and stringing me along to see how much I've figured about his business with Abby.

But I don't think so. Something in his posture, his slight lean toward me, tells me he really knows nothing about the building on Fifty-first Street or what Abby is doing there.

Here's the tricky part: if I tell him what I know, if I tell him that I've been there and what I saw, I could put Abby in danger.

Sig doesn't deal kindly with people who do business behind his back. True, there's no love lost between me and Abby since she drugged me yesterday, but I'm not crazy about the idea of maybe getting her killed.

I'm not crazy about the idea of maybe getting *me* killed, either, which would be a real possibility if I keep what I know from Sig and he finds out later. Sig always finds out later.

Somehow, I've got to thread this needle. "Okay, whatever new venture you're planning with Abby is none of my business, but I assume you'd want to see the old venture, Nick's bookie operation, keep going. I mean, it's been a moneymaker for you, a good return on your investment week after week. If it stays closed, that gravy train dries up. It can't reopen at the old spot down on Water Street. It would attract too much attention since Nick's murder. Maybe Abby's looking for a new spot."

"On East Fifty-first Street?"

I don't answer, just shrug.

"Perhaps she is," he says in a way that's far from approving. "How did you find out about it, Cantor?"

Another needle to thread, and keep that needle from drawing blood from Mike and Freddie, and even Chickie. "C'mon, Sig," I say, giving him my best streetwise attitude, "you know how word gets around on the street, even if it doesn't make it all the way up here to the penthouse. And you also know I'll never give up who I heard it from. They'd never trust me again if I did, and neither would you. Nobody likes a snitch."

"No," he says, drawing it out, "nobody likes a snitch."

We're at an impasse, neither of us getting what we want from the other.

I already lead a risky life. I might as well kick that risk into higher gear. "Look, Sig, I'm going to find out who killed Nick and why, whether you like it or not. I'd love your help, but even without it, it won't stop me. All I ask is that you take the roadblocks off."

"And if I don't?"

"It still won't stop me."

"You know, Cantor, you have not changed at all since you were an annoying little thief back in Coney Island. You were always underfoot. You still are."

Nobody seems to know anything about anything. Sig doesn't seem to know what Abby is up to. He might not even know who the thug was who tried to put the squeeze on Nick, and who Nick wound up killing, and who Sig's crew wound up disposing. The cops don't know who murdered Nick. Worse, they don't care. And Sig doesn't care. And Abby doesn't care. And to tell you the truth, I'm not sure how much Mike, Freddie, or Chickie care. Oh sure, they all gave me the sad spiel, and Chickie gave me a song-and-dance about wanting to help me find the killer, but Abby's their boss now, and as soon as her dough fattens their wallets, Nick Fortunato will be just a guy they used to work for.

I don't want to hear another word from any of them about what a great guy Nick was, what a talented operator he was, or any of that crap. All of it is just crap if no one cares that he was tossed out a window, that he died broken on the sidewalk, wasn't even granted a decent funeral, his body burned and his ashes tossed into the oblivion of the East River. All those hearts and flowers from Nick's loyal employees are just crap if no one gives a damn who killed him, as long as the consequences don't fall on them. Or better yet, there be no consequences at all.

It's time to stop asking questions no one will answer, either because they don't want to or they can't. It's time to put a crack in the wall of silence.

These thoughts come with me during the long ride down the elevator from Sig's penthouse, across the lobby and out to Fortieth Street, and into a phone booth on the corner of Sixth

Avenue. They jangle around in my head as insistently as the jangle of my dime dropping down into Ma Bell's coffers. Those thoughts fuse to a fine point as I dial the number for the one guy whose recent brush with death might make him ready to crack.

"Connect me to Lieutenant Adair," I say to the desk sergeant.

Adair comes on the line with a brusque, "Homicide. Adair."

"You get any information on Stang and Colnick, other than they have records as long as an opera but never served much time?"

"Gold?"

"Stang and Colnick," I press, "what do you have in your files that I don't already know? Like who hired them."

Adair's annoyed *tsk* crackles through the phone line. "I know better than to ask how you found out about their records," he says. "But no, I don't know who hired them. At least not for last night's shenanigans. They've been associated now and then with various local outfits up in Albany, but they're not locals themselves. They migrated up there. Stang was from the tougher parts of Manhattan's West Side, knocked some heads for the old Irish mob. Colnick was originally from Brooklyn, was a gun for 'Kid Twist' Reles and Murder, Incorporated until the DA's office finally broke the outfit back in '41. Other than that, the sheets on them are long but skimpy, with prison time nothing but a joke. You know the deal, Gold. They're—were," he adds, nearly choking on it—"they were connected guys. Look, it's not a good idea for me to ask too many questions about them. Department brass might want to know why. And after last night"—he can barely get it out, choking on the words and the memory—"what the hell am I supposed to tell them?"

I'm never one to give the badge-boys much if any credit for anything, least of all playing the game on the up and up. But I have to admit that on the whole they're a pretty brave bunch. They have to be. Lots of very dangerous people want to kill them. I could probably name you a dozen of my immediate acquaintance who would do the deed if they could get away with it. But right now, Lieutenant Liam Adair, brave member of the Homicide Division, the police department's most feared squad, sounds close to losing his lunch.

Adair's jitters might be that crack in the wall I'm looking for. "Then it's time to get out from under the hammer, Lieutenant," I say. "Meet me at Nick Fortunato's apartment."

"What? Are you nuts? You're the last person I need to hear from or run around with, Gold. You're nothing but trouble in a fancy suit."

"Uh-uh. You've got it wrong, Adair. I'm the only one who can make sure that trouble won't stick to you. Listen, after last night, we're joined at the lapels whether we like it or not, and I know you don't like it any more than I do, which is not at all. But someone tried to kill us, either because I was with you or you were with me, or maybe they wanted both of us. Whoever hired them—"

Adair cuts me off. "I wouldn't be surprised if it was your pal Sig Loreale. I don't care how much the department wants me to work with the guy, I wouldn't trust him to help a blind old lady across the street. And I won't put it past him to have me knocked off after he's through with me." There's enough acid in his every word to eat through his desk.

"Actually, it wasn't Sig," I say. "Turns out he's never heard of Stang or Colnick, but you can bet your last dime he'll make it his business to find out."

"Jeez!" he says, almost spitting it. "You told him about last night? Are you *trying* to get me killed, Gold?"

"I left your name out of it. Wise up, Adair. Last night's escapade in the Staten Island swamps is somehow either tied up with whatever is going on with that business I bumped into at Mom Sheinbaum's place, or with Nick's murder. With the turns things are taking, we might not survive digging into both of them, so let's at least get to the bottom of one of them."

His breath through the phone gets heavier, louder, until it slowly settles down. He's calmer, the nerveless homicide cop again. "Gimme Fortunato's address."

Chapter Eighteen

Adair's already at Nick's door when I get off the elevator and walk along the hall.

"You have a key to the place?" he says.

I give him a smile he doesn't appreciate but one that makes me feel good. He likes my smile even less when I pull my small case of lockpicks from my suit jacket pocket.

"I should've known," he says.

"You going to arrest me for illegal entry, Lieutenant?"

"Too much paperwork. I'll wait until you do something big time, something worth the paperwork. Now, drop the jokes and let's go inside, where you'll tell me why you want me here."

We enter the apartment, step inside the living room, where Adair lets out a whistle between his teeth. "Nice place," he says. "The bookie business was good to Nicky Fast Hands. Rent on this joint must be a pretty penny, and the furniture wasn't cheap, either. This living room looks like it should be on the cover of one of those decorating magazines I see on the rack at my corner newsie. Can't say I'm crazy about all this super modern furniture, though."

"I peg you as a tufted-sofa-and-easy-chair kind of guy," I say.

"Yeah, nice and comfy. Homey, not like that coffee table. A coffee table should have normal lines, y'know, four corners, and not look like someone lost a kidney. Not that I could afford any of this stuff anyway. Not on a cop's salary."

"Then become a bookie," I say, having fun kidding him.

"Very funny, Gold. Maybe you should get out of the criminal racket and go be a comedian on the Ed Sullivan television show."

"You never know, Lieutenant."

I look around, do my best not to fall prey to that pit-of-the-stomach feeling I had when I arrived the other night for Nick's birthday, when Nick wasn't here and I knew something was very wrong. The bloodstained carpet told me so.

I turn away from Adair, don't let him see my jaw tighten, or hear me swallow hard while I get myself back on an even keel, able to look at the living room again.

Everything in the living room is as it should be. Nothing is out of place. The couch's red-and-light-gray striped upholstery is still straight as rails. The racing form that had been haphazardly lying around on the couch the night I was here is now gone. The wine glasses that Nick had set out on the coffee table are gone, too. The logs in the fireplace are carefully stacked. There's not a speck of dust on the furniture.

The place was never this neat when Nick was still alive, puttering around on the carpet in his stocking feet. The whole scene gives me the willies. Most unsettling, though, is the absence of the bloodstain at the foot of the coffee table.

Sig's handiwork. When his boys removed the dead thug, they also removed every trace of what happened here. They must've scrubbed like mad to get that bloodstain out of the carpet. The image of a couple of tough guys on their hands and knees in overcoats and shoulder holsters scrubbing like washerwomen is one that will keep me amused for a long time.

"What are you smirking at?" Adair says. "And what's so interesting about that spot under the coffee table? It certainly has your attention. So I ask you, Gold, what haven't you told me?"

He doesn't wait for an answer, just bends down and slides his fingers along the carpet at the foot of the table. His hand stops. His fingers rub a tiny spot by the table leg. When he stands up again, he's rubbing tiny red spots between his thumb and forefinger, and looking at me.

Every once in a while I have to remind myself that Adair is the smart variety of cop.

He looks again at the tiny specks of red on his fingers. "I guess someone didn't clean up so good," he says. "And something tells me these aren't flecks of dried paint on my fingers."

If picking Nick's lock wasn't enough for Adair to bother with the paperwork he'd have to deal with after arresting me, he looks at me now as if finding evidence of a killing might be worth that paperwork after all. "It's time you told me why you want me here, Gold."

It sure wasn't for him to find specks of dried blood.

And it sure wasn't for him to say, "Someone died here, and it was a rough death. But it wasn't Nicky Fast Hands Fortunato. He died in the Bronx. The Coroner's report said he died from the impact of falling out the window, his bones smashed and his skull crushed when he hit the ground."

Just hearing Adair say it brings back the gruesome sounds of Nick hitting the pavement: the thump of his body, the crack of his skull. The memory makes it hard for me to speak, hard to get out sounds that are words and not sobs. But I won't break down in front of a cop. I won't give the Law any hint of weakness that they could clobber me with later, so I manage to say, "Adair," as easy and normal as I can, "you're a homicide cop. You must've seen your share of death."

He gives that a heavy nod. "And you're no stranger to it yourself, Gold," he says. "Not with the upstanding crowd of crooks and killers you run with." Whatever sympathy he might've had for me over the murder of my old friend is buried in his cop's disgust for my life.

I light a smoke, let the tobacco quiet my irritation at Adair's crummy opinion of my life and the people in it. When the tobacco finally cools my urge to smack him around, I say, "Someday, Adair, when you're sitting at your desk, looking over those files of paperwork you hate so much, maybe you'll open a file and read about the murder of some poor schnook on the street and your heart will stop, because the victim is a schnook you knew, a schnook you liked and cared about. I hope it doesn't happen to you, Adair, because it's a lousy feeling, a pain deep in the gut that I wouldn't wish on anybody, not even a cop." I take a deep drag of the smoke, and realize my hand is shaking. It's shaking not only in anger but from that lousy feeling I warned Adair about. The pain of Nick's murder is in my soul, burrowing so deep it may never go away. It even sparks an old pain, one that never really healed and that twists through me now: the long ago murder of my lost Sophie.

None of that is any of Adair's business. I tighten up to quiet my shakes.

"You owe me, Adair," I say. "After last night, you owe me one helluva favor, and you know it."

He knows it, all right. It's all over his face how much he knows it. He knows I wiped clean his involvement in the killings of Stang and Colnick. He knows—even without having seen me do it—that I drowned the evidence in the swamp. And he knows that if I ever spill the story and it gets back to Police Department brass, his career is over, with a good chance his ass will end up in Sing Sing prison to spend the rest of his days among big guys who hate his cop guts.

The look on his face makes me almost pity him. What's on my face is a different story.

"Why are you smiling?" he says.

"Because, unlike you, Lieutenant, if I end up in prison, the women in my cellblock won't hate me. Hell, I'll fit right in. And if my cellmate is a cutie-pie, we might even become an item, if you catch my drift." My smile now is toothy and rakish.

He's not crazy about my joke, and even less crazy about it that I've got him over a barrel. But he's a cop through to his marrow, so it doesn't surprise me when he says, "What's the favor, Gold?" with the practiced tough tone they must've taught him in the Police Academy.

"Simple," I say. "I want your cop's eyes to look around the place and see if you can spot anything I might've missed. I want you to see anything that doesn't look right, sniff out anything that doesn't smell right. In other words, I want you to be a homicide cop, use the cop brain that led you to find the blood flecks on the carpet. I want you to help me solve Nick's murder."

"Oh, is that all?" he says, pushing his hat back on his head and wiping his lips with the back of his hand as if trying to wipe away a bad taste. "You want me to go against department orders and put my career on the line for a bookie who had no more respect for the badge than you do? Someone's been spiking your whiskey with daydream juice, Gold."

"Who's been spiking yours?" I snap back. "You've been believing your own daydreams if you think Nick's murder and everything that's happened since won't come back to bite you. You know this isn't going away, Adair, no matter how deep the department—and yeah, Loreale—wants to bury it."

His sigh is so heavy I half expect to see his body swell up like a balloon. But his footsteps around the room are light, the careful steps of a homicide cop at the scene of a killing. "And in return," he says, his words tight, almost hissing, "you'll tell me what went on here, because you know what went on here, Gold. You know who died here and why."

"Sure, I'll tell you, and you won't like one bit of it, but you'll understand why you need me along. Because I can get to places and people you can't."

He gives that an uneasy nod. "And I can get into files you can't."

"We understand each other."

"I wouldn't say that, Gold. I'll never understand why you live the way you do, why you dress the way you do. I'll never understand your sick love life."

That's the second time I'm tempted to slap him around. But it's just as much of a bad idea now as it was the first time. It's the sort of idea that can land me behind bars, paperwork be damned.

I unclench my fists at my sides before Adair even notices. "You don't know anything about it, Lieutenant," is all I say.

"And I don't want to know. What I *do* want to know is what went on here the night of Fortunato's birthday. You want my help? Start talking."

I finish my smoke, crush it out in the ashtray on the coffee table. I could remind him again that he owes me a favor, or that I could end his career as a cop with one phone call. But that would only stiffen him. Sure, he'd help me find Nick's killer, but he'd have his own knife at my back all the time.

So I forget about rubbing Adair's nose in last night's mutual dirty doings, and sit down on the couch, ready to spill the story of the dead thug. I nod for Adair to have a seat in one of the chairs, but he just makes a face at its sleek design and leans against the fireplace instead, his arms folded, his muscular face set hard.

I tell Adair what Nick told me, that a young punk showed up here, held a .45 on Nick, said he was sent by his employer to tell Nick he had to clear out of his bookie joint on Front Street so that his boss's organization could take over.

"Employer? What employer?"

"According to Nick, the guy didn't say. Anyway, Nick was having none of it. He wasn't the kind of guy to get pushed around. He even laughed in the kid's face, reminded him that

Sig Loreale was Nick's backer, and Sig doesn't take kindly to threats. But now here's the kicker, Adair. The thug told Nick that Loreale's days are numbered, too. Even called Loreale an old geezer. But by now, Nick was getting tired of having that .45 pushed in his belly, so he made a move on the kid to get the gun. In the struggle, the gun went off and the kid went down. The blood flecks you picked up by the coffee table must've been where the guy fell dead. I saw the bloodstain when I arrived."

"And Fortunato was gone? Ran off to that crummy hotel in the Bronx?"

"Don't get ahead of me, Lieutenant. After the kid went down, Nick called Sig, told him what happened, and what the kid said about muscling Nick out of the Front Street operation and his threat against Sig. It was Sig who told him to go to the Cortland Hotel, a fleabag he quietly owns and uses for just such occasions."

"Uh-huh. And how did you know where to find Fortunato?"

I'm not about to tell him that I'd been kidnapped by a guy I'd known in good times and bad since we were kids, so I just say, "He got word to me."

His eyes narrow at my sketchy answer, but he's smart enough not to bother pressing it, knowing he'd get nowhere, and that it doesn't matter anyway. His face resumes its usual cop's stoniness. "And you didn't see anyone else come to Fortunato's hotel room?"

"Nope. And when I left and got back to the street, I didn't see anyone walk into the hotel, either."

"No one in the hall? Nobody?"

"Just a couple of down-and-outs who could barely stand up when they got off the elevator."

"Uh-huh. Tell me about the kid who showed up with a gun at Fortunato's apartment. I suppose the kid didn't give his name."

"Afraid not."

"Did Fortunato say anything else about him? Something that might help identify him?"

"Only that he was a blond kid, thin build, looked more like a California surf bum than a New York gangster. He wore his coat collar up, trying to pass himself off as a tough guy."

Adair stops his pacing around the room and looks at me. "Blond kid, you say?"

"Yeah. Why? Sound familiar?"

"Could be," Adair says. "But the mugshot books are full of blond thugs."

"C'mon, spill, Adair. If you have an idea who the kid was, let me in on it. If I have his name I might be able to track down who hired him, who this mysterious employer is."

"Not so fast, Gold. I'm not about to toss around names of anybody who may or may not be the guy who showed up here. If it's the wrong guy, it just might get him killed. And there's been a little too much of that lately. Which brings me to my next question." Adair goes over to the spot where the thug went down after the .45 went off, looks carefully around the carpet. "What happened to the kid's body? There's been no police report about a body in this apartment, no report from the Coroner's office of a body delivered to the morgue from here on the night the kid died." He turns his attention to me, gives me a smile so self-satisfied it ought to thank his face for the pleasure. "Did Loreale have him dumped somewhere?" he says through that smile.

I'm tempted to go into Nick's liquor supply and pour myself a scotch, take some liquid fortification to deal with questions I'd rather not answer, not when it comes to anything involving Sig. But it's only a bit past noon, my stomach's gurgling for lunch, and booze on an empty stomach would cloud my head more than it would fortify my spine.

It was me, though, who brought Adair in on this adventure, and I can't duck the fact that his questions come along with his cop's smarts.

Best I can do is be careful. "I don't know what happened to the body, Lieutenant. Nick didn't tell me. He probably didn't know, either, just that Sig told him he'd take care of it, and to get himself to the Cortland Hotel."

"Uh-huh. Why do I get the feeling the kid's body is either in a bog in Jersey, or maybe parts of him are."

"I couldn't say, Lieutenant."

"Well, what about Fortunato's body? I didn't see any notice of a funeral."

"I understand he was cremated."

"Is that so? On whose authority? You keep telling me what good friends you and Fortunato were, that you've had each other's backs since you were kids, and yet it's just your *understanding* that he was cremated? Pretty convenient way to get rid of a body, fast. And just where are Fortunato's ashes?"

Adair's relentless probing is getting dangerously close to figuring Sig's involvement, if he hasn't already. It's time to push him off that road. "What difference does it make, Adair? Nick's dead. Somebody tossed him out a window. What happened to his body after that won't tell us a thing about who killed him. We have one lead, a slim one but the only one: the possible identification of the kid who came to Nick's apartment to put the squeeze on Nick and threaten Sig. If you know who he is, or can find out who he is, tell me his name. He lived in my world, Lieutenant, not yours. I stand a better chance of finding out who his so-called employer was a lot faster than you can, if you could find out at all. The citizens of my world aren't known to rat on each other to cops."

He nods, sucks air through his teeth, annoyed at the reality I've just thrown at him. Then he nods again, says, "I'll check the police records," and starts to the door.

"You'll let me know?"

"I'll let you know."

I decide not to leave with Adair, but hang around Nick's place for a while. He doesn't question it. Maybe his sentimental side figures I need some time alone with my memories of Nick, or maybe he just doesn't care. If he figured the first, he'd be right.

Nick's birthday was just a few days ago. Mine's coming up in a few months. We've been cheated out of celebrating both.

There's a phone on a small glass-topped table next to the couch. I call the red-sauce joint where Nick and I always ordered his birthday dinner. I order a spaghetti lunch and a bottle of red wine. The joint doesn't have the pricey Barolo I'd brought for Nick's birthday, but the house red will do. I tell them to deliver the order, and make it snappy. While I wait, I call Judson. "You have anything new for me on who hired Stang and Colnick? It seems they earned their stripes down here, not up in Albany."

"I was hoping you'd call," he says. "Yeah, I traced Colnick back to the old Murder, Incorporated crowd, and Stang was a gun boss with the Irish mob on the West Side."

"So I heard. Adair filled me in. But his police files and arrest records on the two gunmen had nothing which could help me figure who hired them. You have any leads? And were they after me, or Adair, or both of us?"

"I couldn't say who they were after," he says, "whether it was just one of you or both of you, or why, but I dug up some interesting stuff that might help. Evidently they'd worked together before, joined up as a team for hire. But Stang was the smart gun of the two. He'd been second in command to Johnny Gallagher of the old West Side mob. After Gallagher was killed by Tim Dwyer, who pretty ruthlessly cleaned out Gallagher's people, Stang high-tailed it up to Albany and hooked up with various outfits up there. Colnick was already in Albany. He'd moved up there when Murder, Incorporated was taken down by prosecutors here in the city. Anyway, Stang and Colnick formed their partnership, but it was Stang who had the brains. He'd get the contracts, and Colnick was his side gun. That's all I got so far. Any of that help?"

"Maybe," I say, not sure if I'm happy about it, saddened by it, or not surprised. "Good work, Judson. Now, what about Cosmopolitan Realty Holdings? It turns out Sig has nothing to do with it."

"Then it's still a mystery. There's a lot of off-shore lines to follow. So far, all of them end in a tangle I have to pick through, but I'll keep at it," he says. "Anything else?"

"Yeah. You still have contacts among the younger crowd from your street gang days?"

"I try to keep up," he says with a chuckle that's almost silly with enjoyment. "Why do you ask? Anyone you have in mind?"

"Does a pasty-face guy about your age, maybe a little older and with blond hair, ring any bells?"

The line goes quiet for a while. Only Judson's breathing comes through the phone. "Could be," he finally says. "There were a few guys that might fit that description. Anything else to go on?"

"Physically, no," I say. "But the kid I'm looking for might've been the ambitious type. And liked to wave a gun around."

"Mmm, two guys like that come to mind. Tommy Brandt and Archie Nyles. They ran with the Crashers gang over by the West Side docks."

"Any idea what they're doing now?"

"Not a clue. Haven't spoken to either of them since you pulled me off the streets."

"They still in New York or nearby, as far as you know?"

"I guess so. Want me to track them down?"

"Yeah. If one of them is alive and the other one is dead, or at least no one's heard from him in the last few days, let me know which is which."

"What's this about, Cantor? You think one of them killed Nick?"

"Other way around."

The line goes quiet again while Judson spools this in his brain. Then he says, "Where can I reach you? Or will you be coming by the office?"

"I'll be in touch," I say, and hang up.

I take my coat and cap off just in time for a buzz at the door.

I open the door to the lunch delivery guy. He looks me up and down, his eyes wide, like he's just seen something out of a horror movie. I pay him for the lunch and include a hefty tip, which seems to alleviate his repulsion of a dame in a gentleman's navy blue suit. He's still happy to leave, though, as fast as he can.

Such stuff used to hurt my feelings. It doesn't anymore.

I take the bag of food to the kitchen, transfer the well-sauced spaghetti onto a plate, grab silverware, a white cloth napkin, a corkscrew, and take a wine glass from a cabinet. I carry it all on a tray to the coffee table in the living room, then sit down on the couch and put the napkin at my neck. I open the wine, pour a glassful, lift it, and whisper, "Happy Birthday, Nick."

Chapter Nineteen

I phone Adair after I've finished my lunch and taken a last drink of wine. When he comes on the line, I say, "If you haven't found anything yet to identify the kid in Nick's apartment, I can save you a lot of time. See if the department files have anything on a couple of ex-juvenile delinquents, Tommy Brandt and Archie Nyles. They were in the same street gang, the Crashers, when they were kids."

"I can tell you about one of them: Brandt. He's a hated name around here. Cop killer. He's up in Sing Sing, doing a fifteen-to-life stretch for the murder of a rookie cop from this precinct." He doesn't so much say the words as spit them.

"Lieutenant," I say, my tone rather jollier, "that's the best news I've heard all day."

"You have a warped sense of humor, Gold."

"Let's just say I get a kick out of it when something finally goes my way. Like finding out that the other guy, Archie Nyles, might just be our dead blond boy. Lieutenant, how do you feel about a little trip up the Hudson?"

"To talk to Brandt about Nyles? I don't need you along for that, Gold. I've interrogated hundreds of lowlife scum like him."

"I'm sure you have, Lieutenant," I say through a small but

cynical laugh I can't quite hide. "But do you really think a cop killer is going to open up to a cop?"

Adair's sigh comes through the phone with equal amounts of frustration and annoyed resignation. "You still at Fortunato's place?"

"Yeah."

"I'll pick you up in fifteen minutes."

I call Judson back, tell him Brandt's in Sing Sing, so he doesn't have to bother about finding him. "And Adair and I are going up there to talk to him, see what he knows about Nyles. Just in case he clams up, go ahead and see what you can find out about Nyles's life after his teenage gang days, or what he was up to lately."

After the call, I clean up the kitchen and wait downstairs for Adair to pick me up.

Up the river they call it when the Law sends someone to prison, and Sing Sing has the distinction of originating the phrase way back in the 1890s. The joint is about thirty miles north of New York City, straight up the Hudson River, on a bank of the river with views more suitable for a pricey resort hotel than a maximum security fortress hosting the toughest of the state's tough guys. Sing Sing also boasts a death house with an electric chair that goes by the morbidly jaunty name of Old Sparky.

Adair's badge and ID gets us inside the prison without the red tape of an appointment. We stop at the fortified entry booth, whose steel walls are painted a gummy gray-green designed, I'm sure, to deaden the senses, and whose windows are thick, bulletproof glass. The guards inside the booth look me over in a way that's even less welcoming than the paint. Maybe they don't like my getup, especially my suit. Or maybe they don't like it that I have no shame in wearing the suit. Funny thing is, I feel naked, not because of the way the guards look at me, but because Adair, the smart cop, figured I might be carrying a piece and told me to leave it and the rig in the car. When I asked him about his own piece, he grunted a laugh and told me they'll tag and hold his but arrest me for mine. I dutifully left my gun in the car.

When Adair finishes the sign-in and the request form to interview inmate Thomas "Tommy" Brandt, and slides it through the pass-through, he also hands over his service revolver to be picked up when we sign out.

One of the guards, a young guy, comes out of the booth and walks directly to me. "The cop here is clear," he says. "But you're a civilian, so I gotta frisk you." He suddenly looks uncomfortable, but I'm not sure if it's because he's iffy about me, or that the other guys in the booth are laughing.

Adair says, "Just a second, Officer. Don't female employees search female visitors?"

The guy points at me, his eyebrows way up, his eyes big and round. "You're a female?" he sneers.

"How badly do you want to find out?" I say.

Adair, annoyed at me, the guard, and the guards laughing in the booth, puts his arm between me and the officer. "I'll vouch for my colleague here on behalf of the New York City Police Department that she's not carrying any weapons. Now cut the shenanigans, and let us through." He says this last with a hard stare at the guards in the booth. They stop laughing.

One of the guards buzzes for entry, and a big, gray steel door in front of us swings open.

Noise hits us hard and loud: shouts, laughter, clangs, yells, and various other noises I can't make out but add to the overall racket made by men shut away for hours at a time, years at a time. I suppose the women's prison further upstate is just as noisy, but maybe the noises are different. Maybe angrier. Maybe sadder.

Two guards accompany Adair and me through the prison. They carry big nightsticks, the kind that cracks heads and breaks bones. We're veered away from the cellblocks, and into a long hallway that's lit only by bare overhead bulbs in wire cages. The hallway isn't especially narrow but one can almost feel the thick walls on either side of us, confining us. The claustrophobic feel of the hallway is made worse by the presence of more guards with nightsticks posted every few yards.

We finally arrive at our interview room and go inside. It's a gray-green box with a two-way mirror and a high window allowing light in but too high for a view. The mere presence of daylight teases freedom.

A metal table with two facing chairs is in the middle of the room. There are two doors: the one we entered by, and another across the way. It opens, and Tommy Brandt, escorted by a guard, enters the interview room. Brandt's blue denim regulation shirt and pants are stiff from the prison laundry. As a high-security prisoner doing time for murder, he's shackled at the ankles and handcuffed at his wrists. He's thickly built, and his prison-cropped blond hair makes him look bald. His round face is pale as porridge, and his squinty brown eyes, like slits in a pillow, are empty of all feeling. I wonder if his feelings died as a result of being locked up, or if he never had any feelings at all.

The guard escorting him continues to hold him by the arm as he leads him to a chair on one side of the table, where Brandt sits down.

The guard says, "I'll be right in there"—he points to the two-way mirror—"with another officer. If this guy gives you any trouble, we'll see it and we'll be right in."

Adair smiles and says, "Thank you, Officer. Keep the intercom off, though. This is a conversation on behalf of the NYPD. We wouldn't want anything to happen to inmate Brandt or to my associate," he nods to me, "as a result of anything that's said here. The NYPD will hold you directly responsible." Adair isn't smiling anymore.

The guard's resentment seeps through his uniform like a noxious cloud. He says nothing but turns too sharply on his polished brogues and heads for the door.

Adair sits in the chair opposite Brandt. I stand against a wall behind Adair.

Brandt says to Adair, "You look familiar."

"Adair. Lieutenant Liam Adair."

"The name don't mean nothin' but the face," he says, sneering, "yeah, I know you. You was at my trial. You was part of the bunch that wanted me to go to the chair." His lips purse like he wants to spit in Adair's face, but a glance at the two-way mirror changes his mind. "Whatever you're here for, I ain't talkin' to you."

I step to the table, say, "Then maybe you'll talk to me."

"Who the hell are you?" he says, and frowns at me like he's having a hard time figuring what's in front of him. "And *what're* you? Some kinda she-he?"

"My name's Cantor Gold."

He looks me over, his empty brown eyes a bit less empty for a second. There's a flash of a spark in them. "So you're Cantor Gold. I hearda you. You steal stuff."

"I'd appreciate it if you wouldn't discuss that in front of our cop friend here." I give him a smile and a wink. Adair gives us a *tsk*. I say, "By the way, Tommy, I'm a good friend of Judson Zane's. Remember him?"

"Should I?" His hard grin lets me know he has no use for cooperation.

"Wiry guy," I say. "Glasses. You probably tried to beat him up when you ran with the Crashers and he was with the Dockside Boys. Maybe he surprised you."

Brandt puts his hand to his face like he's soothing a smash to the jaw. He quickly puts his hand down again, burying what

I'm guessing is a humiliating memory of skinny, brainy, teenage Judson Zane out-maneuvering the husky Tommy Brandt, and beating the crap out of him during a gang rumble.

Brandt puts on a tough act. "Yeah, sure, I remember him," he says, and forces a laugh. "How is old four-eyes?"

"He's not in prison and he's making very good dough. I know, because I pay him."

Brandt kicks the belligerence into high gear. "You didn't come here to jabber about Judson. So just why are you here?"

"Hey, no need to get all tough-guy on us," I say, and put my hands up in "don't shoot" style. "You look like a guy who can hold his own in the yard." I count on the idea—well, hope, anyway—that flattery might get me somewhere. "We're just here to ask about another guy down your memory lane. You remember Archie Nyles? He was with you in the Crashers."

He leans across the table, looks past Adair and up at me, his handcuffs clanging on the tabletop. "You ever do time in the women's joint up in Bedford, Gold?" he says through a smile so lewd it could add time to his sentence just for intent.

Adair says, "Not yet," before I can get a word in, and enjoying it more than I'd like.

Brandt says, "Well, lemme give you a little advice for when you finally get sent up. Information don't come free. You gotta come across with somethin' good for me, or I never heard of no Archie Nyles."

"How about this?" I say. "From what I've heard from my less fortunate friends, cartons of cigarettes are considered good coin around here. How about I send you a couple of cases. You'll have enough to trade for whatever favors you want from the other guys for months."

"Don't make me laugh!" he says, but laughing anyway. "I can get plenty of cigarettes, easy, any time. Nah, you ain't got what I need, Gold, but this guy," he looks hard at Adair, "he can get me what I want. And what I want is outta here. I got a birthday commin' up next month. I'd love to celebrate it in my old neighborhood with my old pals."

Adair, stonier than I've ever seen him, leans toward Brandt. "Archie Nyles," he says, his tone so icy it even makes my bones shiver.

It has no effect on Tommy Brandt, though. I guess he's dealt with hard-as-nails guys every day here. Compared to them, Adair's an amateur.

But Adair has a power even the toughest guys in here don't, and he lords that power over Brandt. "Archie Nyles," Adair says again. "That's the price of any goodwill I feel like giving you."

Brandt isn't going down, though. "Make me a deal, cop."

Adair leans back in his chair. "*If* your information is good, I'll see what I can do about getting your parole hearing sooner than fifteen years. How do you like ten?"

"Ten ain't a good number."

I'm starting to see and hear something Adair can't. He may have interrogated dozens of thugs during his years as a cop, but interrogating them isn't the same as speaking their language.

"Lieutenant," I say, "mind if I have a seat?"

Adair turns and looks up at me, his expression telling me that I have a lotta nerve. But he reads something on my face that makes him think again, and he gets up from the chair. "Be my guest," he says.

Before I sit down, I signal to him with my eyes, but out of Brandt's sight, to give me and Brandt some space.

Adair looks doubtful, but he walks to another part of the room anyway.

I look directly at Brandt when I sit down. I say, very quietly, "Look, you and I both know that cops can't be trusted. But you can trust me. I can't get your time cut, but maybe I can get you other stuff, stuff that will matter in here. You know what I'm talking about. So you help me, Tommy, and I'll help you. But listen, before we talk about Archie, there's something I have to know. You know the streets, you know its code, you know what keeps us alive out there and what crosses the line. Killing cops crosses the line, so why'd you kill the cop?"

The tough-guy prison inmate of a moment ago slowly becomes the young punk vulnerable to every hurt and danger of the streets. His eyes are tinged red, not just with some long held misery, but with anger. I know that anger. I've felt it before. I felt it last night at the swamp.

Brandt leans across the table, as close to me as possible. "He was a lousy, rotten snitch," he says, almost whispering. "That's why. Thought he was a big deal in that blue uniform. Thought that uniform gave him the right to snoop where he wasn't welcome and snitch on what he saw there. Well, one day he snitched on somethin' he saw but got all wrong and when word got aroun' to the wrong ears it ended up with a bullet in my mom's back. My mom was a saint. She never did nothin' wrong. She just got in someone's way without even knowin' it, and all because of that lousy cop." His steel bracelets rattle when he lifts his hands to wipe his eyes. He does it fast, pushing back the tears he'd rather die than let anyone, especially Adair, see. When he pulls himself together, he keeps talking. "So one day, I waited for the creep to walk the neighborhood, make his rounds. When I saw him, I called him into an alley and plugged him. He deserved it. You know that, Gold. You know that."

I don't know if Adair heard any of it. If he did, he's playing it cool, letting me keep waltzing with Tommy Brandt. If he didn't hear it, he never will. Like Tommy said, I know the code.

Before Brandt leans back in his chair again, he says, "You better make good on getting me stuff, Gold."

"Tell me about Archie Nyles, and you'll have my word." I give him a nod.

He understands, and nods back.

He says, "Whaddya wanna know about Nyles?" He's not whispering anymore.

"You have any idea what he's been up to since you two left the Crashers? Especially lately?"

"Well," he starts, clearly enjoying being needed, something he probably hasn't felt since his gang days, maybe not even before that, "Archie always had dreams of doin' big stuff. He wanted to be a big man with a gun, y'know? Figured maybe he'd be a gun for hire. I think it might've worked out for him because the last time I saw him he was braggin' about workin' for some fancy dame."

I never saw that coming. I do my best to hide the shock. Even Adair makes a move back to the table, but I give him a quick glance. He understands, hangs back again.

I say, "This fancy dame have a name? Or what she does?"

"Archie didn't give me a name, just that she was in the bookie racket."

Chapter Twenty

As soon as we're in Adair's squad car, before he even turns on the ignition, he gives me a hard look. "You know the woman Brandt was talking about, don't you. The woman who might've employed Nyles to put the squeeze on Fortunato. I saw your face go white as curdled milk when he said she was in the bookie racket, so don't play stupid with me, Gold."

That code Tommy Brandt and I know so well, the one we live by if we want to stay alive, is staring me in the face right now.

Adair says, "Well, who is she? Look, you say you want to nail your pal Nick's killer. My guess? Either the woman pushed him out that window or knows who did."

"She couldn't have killed Nick," I say. "Not unless she was hiding in the walls of that fleabag hotel. I never saw her in the hotel. She didn't walk into the place when I was there, or I would have seen her in the hall when I left Nick's room. And no one walked into the hotel as I walked out."

"Then she knows who killed him." Adair starts the car, puts it in gear, drives us away from the prison and onto the highway back to town.

"Maybe she does and maybe she doesn't," I say, sick to my stomach that Abby could be part of Nick's killing. Or maybe I just don't want to face just how ruthless Abby can be.

"Listen, Gold, either you tell me who she is, or I'll sweat it outta the dirty cops down on Front Street who've been on the take." Now it's Adair who looks sickly. I bet he's never even accepted a free doughnut from a coffee shop. But cops have their code, too, and even a clean cop like Adair won't snitch on a dirty one, no matter how sick to *his* stomach it makes him. "They've probably seen her at the bookie joint," he says, "probably did a little business with her. Either way, I'll get her name."

"But you'd rather get it from me," I say.

He grasps my meaning, knows I get it that he doesn't want to go up against the cop code.

I say, "Even if I tell you who she is, she'll never talk to you, Adair. Not without a battering ram of a lawyer present. You'll get nowhere." I don't tell him that if it ever got back to Sig that Abby had even been approached by the police, it's a good bet Sig wouldn't wait to hear if she clammed up or broke under questioning, spilling secrets between them he doesn't want spilled. I'm sure Abby wouldn't talk, but Sig might want a guarantee she'd never talk again.

Adair says, "She'll talk to you?"

"I stand a better chance."

"Is that so? And why is that? Oh, yeah. She's a 'special friend' of yours?" The way he says it, I want to wash his mouth out with soap.

"I feel sorry for you, Lieutenant," I say, "spending all your nights alone."

He doesn't say another word. Just drives down the highway, his hands tight on the steering wheel.

To escape the tension between us, I get lost in the view of the Hudson River. The thin, blue-gray November light of early evening puts a steely sparkle on the water. The New Jersey hills across the river fade into a purple silhouette. The darkening scene reflects my mood.

When we finally cross the Henry Hudson Bridge at Spuyten Duyvil and into Inwood at the northernmost tip of Manhattan, it's time to break the tension, time to get back to business with Adair. "Look, Lieutenant, we've played square with each other so far. If you have any hope of getting information from the woman Nyles might've worked for, or even making a charge against her stick, you'll have to play square with me a little longer."

He doesn't answer. He doesn't say a thing until we get off the West Side Highway and back on the city streets. "And you'll play square with me?"

"As long as you don't look over my shoulder," I say, "or let any other cops tag along, either."

"And you'll tell me what you find out?"

"I'll tell you anything I get about Nick's murder."

"That answer's a little too slick, Gold."

"It'll have to do, Lieutenant." I tell him to let me out at the next corner. After I get out of the car and Adair drives away, I head for the subway entrance on the next block instead of hailing a cab, which Adair could follow. He doesn't need to know where I'm going.

It's a little before five-thirty when I arrive in the alley next to the building on Fifty-first Street. It's dark in the alley, the only light from the open door of the building, the same side door Mike Landers and Freddie Holmes took me through last night. The light throws a yellow rectangle along the ground, and shines on four guys in work clothes who load various pieces of construction equipment, lumber, and toolboxes into a truck. CONNOR & SONS CONSTRUCTION and a telephone number are painted on the door of the truck's cab.

I walk into the building before any of the workmen, busy with their equipment, have a chance to notice me.

The janitor I saw yesterday is still inside. I repeat Mike's ritual of slipping the guy ten bucks to look the other way while I go along the same hallway I went along last night with Mike and Freddie. I use my lockpicks to open the door at the end of the hall, then make my way down the stairs and into the garage. The door marked NO ENTRY that Mike unlocked last night is open now, the big room beyond it, the room where Abby wants to open her nightclub-cum-bookie joint, is lit up by the overhead glass-domed lamps.

Inside, it's clear that Abby's not wasting any time in getting things up and running. Signs of construction are everywhere, especially toward the back, where wood-framing for a wall separating the nightclub from the bookie operation is well underway.

Two workmen are finishing sweeping sawdust into trash cans. When they see me walk in, one of them says, "Hey, whaddya doin' here?" Getting a better look at me, he gives me a lip-curling snicker, while the other guy says, "Pervert," more or less under his breath but just loud enough for me to hear.

I don't give a damn. If I ever see these guys again, maybe I'll put my fist in their faces and strike a blow for freedom, but I have a more immediate concern right now. "Abby O'Neill around?" is all I say.

One of them says, "Who the hell is Abby O'Neill?"

Either the guy's lying, or these guys really have no idea who's contracted this job. If it's the latter, I have to hand it to Abby. I've always figured she's smart, but maybe I didn't know how smart. She knows how to play the deep game.

Chapter Twenty-One

Abby opens her apartment door seconds after I buzz. She's surprised to see me, though not very much.

She's decked out for what she'd obviously planned as a quiet evening at home: violet satin lounging pants and top with thin blue pinstripes, and a matching military-style robe. On any other woman the robe might be an overstatement, but describes Abby to a T: serene, self-assured, alluring as the mythical siren inviting the unsuspecting to their deaths.

But I'm not among the unsuspecting. At this point, I suspect Abby of everything.

Her smile has the affectation of the perfect hostess. "Come in, Cantor. It's still cocktail hour, and I just mixed a shaker of martinis. Care for one?"

"I'll stick to scotch, thanks." I follow her through the vestibule and into the living room.

"Have a seat," she says and walks to a liquor cart against a far wall. A torch lamp next to the cart sends a sparkle onto the bottles and glasses, and a sheen on Abby's dark, wavy hair. The rest of the room is shadowy, with faint slats of light coming through the window blinds from streetlamps twenty-one stories below.

I ditch sitting in the rust-colored chair I sat in yesterday to avoid its annoying reminder of Abby tricking me into a drugged stupor. I just toss my overcoat and cap onto the chair, more or less hiding it from my sight, and sit at one end of the couch instead.

Abby pours me a tumbler of scotch and a martini for herself. She gives me my drink, and sits at the opposite end of the couch, her body descending in a smooth glide. Slats of pale light from the window slither along her satin loungewear.

We face each other, size each other up, and each take a sip of our drinks. After her swallow, Abby flicks her tongue along her upper lip, savoring the film of the martini, then says, "I assume you didn't come here for a social evening, Cantor. More's the pity. So ask me what you came to ask me."

"Was Archie Nyles your boy?"

If it wasn't for my love of women and my deep appreciation of how subtly their faces can convey feelings or hide them, I might miss the almost imperceptible tightening around Abby's eyes. "What do you mean, 'my boy'?"

"So you do know him?" I say.

With a resigned sigh, her face relaxes again, and she's again comfortable in her own skin. "There's no point in playing games, is there," she says.

"There never is, Abby."

She gives that an annoyed side-smile but follows it with a stoic shrug. "All right, yes, I know Archie."

"Not the nicest guy to know, or so I've heard. What exactly does he do for you?"

"Odds and ends," she says unconvincingly and not caring whether I believe her or not. She takes another sip of her martini.

"And I suppose you haven't seen him in a few days," I say. "What's the matter, Abby? You look a little puzzled."

"It's just an odd question." She takes a cigarette from the small brass box on the coffee table, lights it with a matching lighter. Her exhale of smoke curls in front of her face, her nervous breath puncturing the smoke, twisting it. "Why would you know or care whether I've seen him or not?"

"Because I know you haven't. Because he's dead."

Her grip on her martini glass tightens. Her fingers on her cigarette stiffen. Her eyes drill into me. "Did you—?"

"Kill him?" I finish for her. "Why would you think that, Abby? Maybe because Nick Fortunato was a good friend of mine and I figure you sent Nyles to put the squeeze on Nick? Or maybe you think I figured Nyles tossed Nick out that hotel window and I took my revenge? Oh, and it wasn't a good idea to try to put the squeeze on Loreale through Nyles. Not a good idea at all. You're in business with Loreale, at least for the moment," I say half smiling, half sneering, "so you really ought to know that crossing him is a dangerous gamble. And no, I didn't kill Archie Nyles."

She sits up slowly, crushes her smoke in an ashtray on the coffee table, puts down the nearly empty martini glass, looks at me and then looks out across the room, staring at nothing. She's got the tense, blank stare of someone facing a firing squad. "Was it Sig?"

"Nope," I say. "Archie Nyles was the rare guy Sig didn't turn into a corpse. It was Nick who killed Nyles—well, sort of. Your boy made the mistake of shoving his gun into Nick's belly. Y'know, for all the years you worked with Nick, I guess you never caught on that Nick Fortunato wouldn't stand for anyone trying to push him around. Nick didn't like having that .45 in his belly, so he grabbed the gun, or tried to. He and Nyles struggled for it, the gun went off, and the bullet tore into young Mr. Nyles."

"Nick told you this? Oh, yes, you were at that hotel where he was killed. How did you know where to find him?"

"That's my business. Mine and Nick's. What matters, Abby, is that your scheme went off the rails. So okay, you weren't the one who pulled the trigger that killed Nyles, and I'm pretty sure you weren't the one who pushed Nick out that window, but you were the cause of both of those deaths. The only way to get their blood off your hands is to peel the skin off."

She closes her eyes for a moment, hiding inside herself, hiding from a danger she hopes won't find her. "Does Sig know any of this?"

"He knows all of it. Sig owns the Cortland Hotel. It was Sig who sent Nick there to hide out. It was Sig who wanted to keep Nick alive."

Abby stares across the room again, her eyes wide, as if looking into an abyss she's calculating how to avoid. I don't know if she's found a way, but she soon comes back to our here and now. "Where's Archie's body?" she says. "I'd like to arrange his funeral."

"Don't bother," I say. "There's no body to bury, unless you find bits and pieces of him scattered who knows where. And yeah, that was Sig's doing." I swallow more of my scotch while I let all this sink into Abby's still calculating brain. After I polish off the rest of my drink, I say, "Now tell me, Abby, how did you know Nick was holed up at the Cortland Hotel in the Bronx? Who'd you send over there to kill him?"

"But I didn't!" There's panic in her voice now. "I had no idea he was there. I'd never heard of the Cortland Hotel until I read about Nick's death in the paper. And I didn't tell Archie to kill Nick, just scare him, soften him up so I could move him out of the operation. Cantor, you've got to believe me!"

"Oddly enough, I do."

Her body relaxes again, the satin robe softly rippling as she lies back deep into the couch. "Look, I never wanted Nick to be hurt," she says. "I didn't want him killed. Even I know that would be a stupid move. I mean, look at all the trouble it's caused, trouble I don't need."

"But I bet you're not sorry Nick's dead. From what I hear, you argued with him plenty to expand the bookie business, but he wasn't buying. You had bigger plans, and Nick stood in your way. Looks like someone did you a favor."

She can't quite hide the pleasure of that convenient reality. She's even more the sultry siren now, comfortable on her couch, comfortable in her place in the world, especially her new, more powerful place now that Nick's out of the way. "All right, yes, it's lucky for me that Nick's dead, but whether you believe me or not, I liked him. I liked him very much. I didn't want him dead, I didn't send Archie to kill him. But Nick *is* dead, life goes on. And so does business."

"I wouldn't be so sure, Abby. After all, who's financing this big operation you're planning over on Fifty-first Street?"

She looks at me as if I'd just said something funny. "I thought you knew," she says.

"I'd figured it was Sig, considering he'd financed Nick. But it's not Sig."

She gives me a half-smile, the kind you give when you're disappointed in someone. "You know, Cantor," she says, "I always pegged you as a class act, doing business on the grand scale with the city's crème de la crème. I've never known you to think small."

"There's nothing small about Sig Loreale," I say. "He's been known to topple governments."

"That was true once, but he's thinking too small for today's action. He's playing it safe. This isn't the old days, Cantor. It's modern times, the atomic age, the rock-'n'-roll age. Sig Loreale is a dinosaur."

"Maybe so," I say. "But didn't they teach you in elementary school that dinosaurs were dangerous predators? They had big, sharp claws and huge teeth and they liked to chew their prey to pieces before they swallow them. So I'd be very careful, Abby, about underestimating this particular dinosaur by going behind his back."

"Thanks for the advice," she says, too flippant for her own

good. "Meanwhile, I'll keep establishing my new business."

"At your own risk."

With a wave of her hand, she tosses that off, too. "I can handle Mr. Loreale. I'm no rookie, Cantor, or have you already forgotten I'm a mob brat, daughter of a gunman for the old Irish mob. I know how the game is played."

It's an argument I'm not going to win. I just hope for Abby's sake it's one I won't lose. "Then you'd better play the game well, Abby."

She gives me a half smile, a little playful, a little seductive, and all calculating. "You volunteering to coach me?"

"What could I possibly teach a mob brat? So let's talk about the money, instead. If it isn't Sig who's putting up the cash for the Fifty-first Street action, who is? Out-of-town money?"

"Oh no, very much New York money," she says, and gets up from the couch. She slowly paces the area, her violet satin loungewear catching the light through the window blinds, the slatted light crisscrossing the outfit's pinstripes. "It's a partnership," she says, turning to me, "partly my own money, much of it hers. The woman thinks big, always has. Maybe you just can't see it."

"I know her?" A queasy feeling creeps into my belly. Agony gnaws at my heart. And a confusion so knotted it clogs my brain. I don't want to think Lily's playing both sides against the rest of us in the middle, doing that mysterious job off the books for Sig and Adair and Mom, and in cahoots with Abby O'Neill, all at the same time.

Abby says, "You know her, all right," enjoying teasing me. "Oh, Cantor, you're a lucky so-and-so and you don't even know it. There are people who give a damn about you."

"Tell me who they are and I'll send them a card next Valentine's Day; that is, if I believed them. Because clearly someone doesn't care about me at all. Someone almost had me killed last night."

Abby gives me a look I don't expect: genuine shock. "What? Who?"

Part of me is relieved it wasn't Abby who arranged the murderous festivities in the swamp, the part that's enjoyed doing a little flirting with her at Nick's bookie parlor, the part that's laughed with the crowd taking bets on who she spends her nights with, the once friendly part that now sees an opening. "Listen, Abby, your money may not be from out of town, but the killers were. You ever hear of a couple of hired guns from Albany named Stang and Colnick?"

"Colnick, uhm, no," she says with a raised eyebrow. "But Stang, Stang, yes, I remember that name. Bill—no, Willy Stang. I remember my dad mentioning him when he worked for the mob. Stang might've been an enforcer, like my dad. What's he doing up in Albany?"

"Escaped the housecleaning of the mob's takeover."

"He tried to kill you?"

"Almost succeeded." I leave Adair out of it. The less Abby knows there's a cop involved, the better. "Seems Stang and Colnick formed their own kill-for-hire partnership after they slipped out of town. Any idea who Stang takes contracts from these days?"

"No. I've never met him. I haven't heard his name since Dad mentioned him years ago."

"Well, never mind that now," I say, abandoning that dead end. "I still want to know whose money is warming your handbag for the Fifty-first Street operation."

"Are you sure you want to know? It might break your heart, Cantor."

My heart's already breaking. I need to hear the truth if I hope to pick up the pieces. It won't be the first time I've had to put my heart back together again. "Tell me."

With an it's-your-funeral shrug, Abby says, "Mom Sheinbaum."

I don't know whether it's the deep relief that she didn't name Lily, or the nonsense about including Mom Sheinbaum among the people Abby says care about me, or maybe it's both that's making me laugh, a booming, pit-of-the-stomach laugh that scares Abby.

I'm still laughing when I get up from the couch, the laugh dwindling to a chuckle as I walk across the living room to the bar cart, getting a kick out of the idea that those rumors about Mom Sheinbaum are true: that she has millions in cash stashed all over the place. She certainly has enough dirt on enough politicians to get Abby's liquor license overnight with just a phone call.

I pour myself a scotch, hold up the martini shaker and ask Abby with a nod if she wants a refill. She shakes her head no.

I carry my drink to the window, look through the Venetian blinds to the nighttime view of Central Park, its old-fashioned lamps sending pools of light along the park's winding paths. If I ever needed a reminder that there's beauty in this sometimes hard and unforgiving city, this view is that reminder. I'm not laughing anymore, but I'm smiling.

I say, "Abby, has Mom ever mentioned the nature of her relationship to Sig?"

"I know she does business with him. And yes, I know the three of you have a long history, since you were a kid, if that's what you mean."

I swallow the rest of my scotch. "In part," I say.

"What's the other part?"

I put my empty glass back on the bar cart, take my coat and cap from the chair. "That's for Mom to say, if she wants to. Good night, Abby."

Chapter Twenty-Two

I call Judson from a phone booth on the corner. It's almost seven-thirty, so I call him at his apartment.

After our hellos, he says, "You're never going to believe who Archie Nyles has been working for: Nick Fortunato's right hand."

"Abby O'Neill. Yeah, I know. Your old pal Tommy Brandt put me on the scent. I just came from her place. She gave me quite a whopper, though. It seems Mom Sheinbaum is fronting a lot of the cash for Abby's new operation. Right under Sig's nose."

I hear Judson's airy whistle between his teeth. "Mrs. Sheinbaum sure plays risky games in her old age. If Loreale finds out . . ." There's no airy whistle this time, just a long, slow breath.

"Yeah," is all I say.

Judson says, "But I finally got a line on Cosmopolitan Realty Holdings. A Wall Street contact of mine helped me plow through a lot of sub-companies and a lot of false names, but at the bottom of it all it looks like the controlling shareholder is some outfit called Opal Investments."

Hearing that name is like bricks falling on my head before they assemble themselves into the shape of an arrow, an arrow that points to only one person.

After Judson and I hang up, I laugh again.

It's a little after eight o'clock when I come up from the subway at Second Avenue and Forsyth Street on the Lower East Side. I grab a quick bite at a delicatessen a block away on Chrystie Street, where the aromas of corned beef, pastrami, and briny pickles are the same aromas a lot of New Yorkers' immigrant grandparents enjoyed not long after they got off the boat.

Sustained by a corned beef on rye with plenty of zesty mustard and the heritage that comes with the sandwich, I walk the few blocks up Second Avenue to Mom Sheinbaum's house. The street's crowded with neighborhood types: the last of the old-time crowd sharing the sidewalk with new immigrants and their babble of languages, and artists moving into the neighborhood for its colorful mix of cultures and its cheap rent. Everyone's savoring the noise and the aromas, everyone's claiming their piece of the night, and enjoying, or at least tolerating, each other.

I'm churning with questions for the old lady as I walk up the front stairs to Mom's door. I ring the doorbell, and out of habit I straighten my cap, overcoat, and tie, and laugh at myself for doing it.

When she opens the door, her hefty form is silhouetted by the light in the vestibule behind her. Only her silvery hair catches any light, a fluffy crown above her round face and bulky body.

She sees me clearly, though. "So what brings you to my door this time?"

"Opal Investments."

The silver-crowned silhouette goes stiff and motionless in the doorway. "You were always smart, *mommeleh*," she says with a rare lilt of approval. "Even when you were a little *pisher* from

Coney Island trying to unload your *tchotchkes*. So I suppose you want to ask me a lotta questions, no?"

"A lotta questions, yeah."

"Well, come inside. I don't have any more honey cake, but how about a nice cup of tea? I have already, hot on the table." She stands aside, ushers me into the vestibule, where I'm nearly blinded by her pink housedress with black polka dots that hangs on her corpulence like a circus tent.

"I'll pass on the tea," I say.

"Suit yourself."

I follow her through the old-fashioned parlor and into the dining room. The heavy mahogany furniture, always polished to a luster, glows softly in the light of two lamps on the sideboard. The flowery porcelain teapot and its cup and saucer glimmer on a silver tray on the table. The scene is lush and lovely, but not enough to make me want a cup of tea. I head for the sideboard instead, open the liquor cabinet, and pour myself a hefty scotch.

Mom sits down in her usual chair at the head of the table. I put my drink down near her, take my cap and coat off and place them on a chair at the side of the table, then sit down at the corner near Mom. "Okay," I say, "what's the story with Opal Investments? Why are you cutting Sig out of your partnership with Abby O'Neill?" I take a swallow of the scotch, watch Mom's small dark eyes narrow, watch her mouth spread slowly into a tight, bitter smile.

"How did you find out?" she says. "Oh, sure, that boy genius of yours, I suppose. The kid with the *klugn kop*."

"Smart me to employ a guy with a smart head."

She enjoys my little verbal joke, gives it a snicker. "He must've done some pretty fancy digging to find out about Opal Investments. I guess it's the name that led you to me."

"It couldn't be anyone else, Mom."

"No, it could not." She lowers her head with a sad, heavy sigh.

"You named it after your daughter."

"May she rest in peace." She raises her head, wipes her eyes with her chubby fingers, her rings glinting in the lamplight. She takes a minute to get through her mourning, then says, "That woman, that Abby O'Neill, she has a *klugn kop*, too. She's smart. Not smart like you. Different. You're smart in the street. She's smart in the bank."

"She has nice things to say about you, too," I say. "So now that we've gotten the mutual admiration out of the way, fill me in on why you're turning your back on Sig. You've known him for years, done business with him for years, but all of a sudden his money's not good enough?"

"It will never be good enough," she says with sharp, quiet spite. "I've waited a long time to get back at him for putting my sweet Opal in danger. She's dead because of him. I don't care how much he says he loved her. He don't know the meaning of love, not a mother's love. I'll never forgive the *momzer*. Never." Her tiny eyes squint, as if she's taking deadly aim. "This business with Miss O'Neill is my chance to get him where it hurts, in his wallet." Her hands are at her eyes again, wiping away tears, but there's a tight set to her mouth. She forces a deep breath, calms herself, and looks at me. "So what's your interest in what business I do with Miss O'Neill?" she says.

"There might be a connection to Nick Fortunato's murder."

"Is that so?"

"It's the people, Mom. Everybody involved in Abby's new business was also involved with Nick's old one. Even Sig was involved with Nick."

"True," she says. "So you think one of us put the finger on him? Listen, *mommeleh*, so maybe you're right. But if you're thinking it was me, put your head back onto your shoulders. I had no beef with Mr. Fortunato."

"You didn't want him out of the way so you and Abby could do bigger business?"

"Miss O'Neill came to me after Fortunato died. For all I know, it was her who had him knocked off."

"She didn't."

"You sure?"

"Pretty sure."

Mom shrugs that away. I guess she doesn't care if Abby is a murderess or not. She serves Mom's purpose, and that's all that matters. "Anyway," she says, "she gave me a spiel about what she had in mind for a new business. It sounded pretty good. She has a head for numbers, that one, a head for money. But you know what I liked best about her spiel?" She's smiling now. There's even a twinkle in her eyes. "Her plans don't include Sig. She's cutting him out. Such a gift that was to me! I didn't ask her why and I didn't care. None of my business. I just saw my chance to stick a knife into that monster Loreale's back, and making a few bucks while I'm at it couldn't hurt."

In all the years I've known Mom, I've seen her hatreds, I've seen her wrath, and I've seen her misery over the loss of her precious daughter. What I've never seen is her fear, and I don't see it now when she should be shaking in her sensible shoes about what Sig might do to her when he finds out.

And then I know, just as Mom knows: he'll do nothing to her. He'll never hurt Esther "Mom" Sheinbaum, the woman who shares his history, his climb from the honky-tonks of Coney Island to the pinnacle of the New York underworld. He'll never lay a finger on the mother of the only woman he ever allowed himself to love.

I feel a sudden chill, the kind of chill you get when you sense death's next target. "What about Abby? Don't you care what Sig will do to her?"

"Why? You sweet on her?" Mom's chuckle isn't chummy. It's not the chuckle of a pal ribbing you about your latest crush. Her chuckle is full of revulsion for my love life. It's not the first time.

"I don't have to be sweet on a woman to care whether she

lives or dies," I say.

"Okay, okay, have it your way. Look, *bubbie*, it's getting late. I'm an old woman. Go home."

"Just answer me two more questions, Mom. What's going on with Lieutenant Adair and that group I barged in on the other day? What's Lily Vardanian got to do with it?"

Mom gives me a look that only someone who's known me since I was a kid could give: a furrowed brow over a mischievous look in her eyes and a cunning smile. "Didn't I teach you anything when you were a little nothin' with a satchel of stolen trinkets on your back? You should know better than to ask me anything about things that are none of your business. But Miss Vardanian . . . hah! She's the one you're sweet on, isn't she. Lotsa luck with that!" Her laugh isn't any friendlier than her chuckle.

"I still have one more question," I say.

"Make it fast."

"Does Abby know anything about the business with Adair, Sig, you, and Lily?"

"If I didn't tell you, why should I tell her? She's nothing to me but revenge and maybe a little cash."

I swallow the rest of my scotch to get rid of the bilious taste suddenly in my mouth. It doesn't help.

I leave without even saying goodbye.

Chapter Twenty-Three

I'm not home five minutes when the phone rings. It's Chickie. "I've been trying to reach you," he says, excited. "I said I'd help you, and that's what I'm gonna do. I got something for you. Listen up."

"Forget the preamble, Chickie. Just tell me what's on your mind."

"Okay, okay, don't be so impatient. Allow me my little theatrics."

"Try that on Abby. Maybe she'll put you in her floor show. You can do your old vaudeville act, complete with costumes and pratfalls. Right now, though, just spill whatever beans you've got, Chickie."

I hear a deep breath at the other end of the line, then, "Okay. Listen, Cantor, Abby had nothing to do with Nick's killing, and I can prove it."

"You're wasting my time, Chickie. I already know that."

"But you don't know the rest of it, and it's blue chip, believe me. I think I know who killed Nick."

"You *think* you know? Based on what?"

"C'mon now, Cantor, you know nothing comes for free. What's it worth to you?"

"It's worth me not coming over to your place and slamming you against a wall." Then I add with a sneery laugh, "Or toss you out a window."

"That's not funny, Cantor. Just for that, I ain't telling you a thing. You want to know who killed Nick? You're on your own." The phone slams down in my ear.

I don't know who to be more annoyed at: Chickie, for giving me the runaround, or myself, for lousing up the chance to get Chickie to give me a name.

He only *thinks* he knows who killed Nick? That's pretty thin soup, but it's more than I have. What am I missing?

I collapse into my living room chair, go over in my mind all the moves I've made after Nick hit the pavement, replay all the conversations I've had with Mike, Freddie, Abby, Sig, Mom, even Chickie. I try to puzzle out who might've sent Stang and Colnick to take out Adair and me, and why.

After all that thinking, I'm still nowhere.

So I take it back to the beginning, to Nick's apartment and the blood on the carpet. Adair and I already had our time with that, which eventually led us to the identity of Archie Nyles, the thug who put the squeeze on Nick. But I realize all those efforts have been after the fact, after Nick's killing.

I take it back further, to the space of time between Nyles's death in Nick's apartment and Nick crashing through the window of the Cortland Hotel.

I get up from the chair and go to the phone. It's almost ten o'clock, but I take a chance.

The desk sergeant tells me Adair's gone for the night. I tell him to call him at home, or get a message to him wherever he is, fast. Tell him to meet me at the Cortland Hotel in the Bronx.

"And just who are you?"

If I give my name, the guy will probably hang up on me. "Just give him the message. He'll know who it is."

Traffic's heavy in my neighborhood, as usual at this hour, with cabs jamming the streets with the after-theater and jazz clubs second-show crowds. It finally thins out further uptown on the West Side Highway and I make it up to the Bronx and the Cortland Hotel in less than an hour.

The hotel's yellow neon ROOMS sign is still flashing on and off, sending its garish staccato along the street.

There's actually a parking spot right in front of the hotel, and I allow myself the fantasy that the Fates are finally having things go my way.

I decide to wait in my car for Adair. If I go up to Nick's room alone, I might step all over some detail that Adair's cop brain could catch, and right now I need his cop brain.

In the meantime, I turn the radio on, figure I'll just relax, close my eyes against the flashing of that ugly yellow light, and let music clear my head until Adair gets here.

But the radio doesn't do me any favors. The song that comes on is the same tune, Sam Cooke's dreamy *You Send Me,* that played on the jukebox at the Green Door Club when I asked Lily to dance. We didn't dance, at least not on the dance floor, and I'm not sure you'd call what we did in her hotel room dancing, though I suppose in a way it was.

Sitting here in my Buick, listening to that tune, remembering that night, I ache for Lily Vardanian.

Adair's knock on my car window jolts me out of my reverie. I'm not sure if it's an invasion or a relief.

"Sorry to disturb your beauty sleep," he says as I get out of the car. "This better be good, Gold, to get me outta my comfortable chair where I was relaxing with a bottle of beer while I watched the *$64,000 Question* on TV and felt like an idiot when I couldn't even answer the two-dollar question."

"They don't have a two-dollar question," I say.

"Just as well," he says. "So what's this all about? What do you think we'll find here that hasn't already been found? The Bronx homicide boys went over this place with a fine-tooth comb."

"But it wasn't your comb, Adair. And it wasn't mine. Look, one or both of us already talked to people who had any connection to Nick, and all we got were fingers in our eyes. Maybe we need to go backward before we go forward, take a good look at where Nick hid out and where he was killed. Maybe we'll find a grain of Manhattan sand the Bronx cops didn't recognize."

He gives that a nod and an "Mm." I must've hit his Manhattan pride button, a feature of Manhattan cops and their occasional snobbery regarding their outer-borough brethren. I press that button again. "So turn on that cop brain of yours, Adair, and show me how Sergeant Liam Adair rose to become Lieutenant Liam Adair."

He pushes his hat back like he's unimpressed by the flattery, but he can't quite hide the smile on his tough face.

We start for the door of the hotel.

"Wait a second," I say, and wander over to the spot where Nick hit the pavement. The chalk outline the Bronx homicide cops drew around Nick's body is scuffed and nearly gone. Only a few small shards of window glass litter the street. They glitter yellow in the flashing sign.

First, the ache for Lily. Now the renewed grief over Nick. My soul is taking a beating.

"Let's go," Adair says. This time his intrusion really is a relief.

I follow him into the hotel.

He stops us in the vestibule. "Any memories stirring up? Like who you might've seen come in or go out?"

"There was no one. I didn't see anyone walk inside, I didn't see anyone leave."

He nods again, and we continue into the postage stamp-size lobby, if you could call that slummy room a lobby. There isn't even a couch or a single chair. I guess the management, one Sig Loreale, doesn't want any loiterers.

The desk clerk, a skinny, seedy-looking guy who looks like he'd hide under the covers in a thunderstorm, is asleep in his chair behind a counter. He could've been asleep for all I know the night I was brought here from Front Street, unconscious from that slam to the back of my head. And I don't remember seeing him when I left the hotel. Then again, I didn't look.

Adair wakes the guy up with a pat to the cheek.

With a sharp, "Huh?" and a phlegmy swallow, the clerk comes to his senses. His face screws up, looks scared when he sees the badge Adair's flipped at him. Then the guy looks at me, looks me up and down, which makes me wonder if he recognizes me, until he sneers at my suit under my open coat, and says, "I didn't know the police department hires perverts."

I guess he was asleep after all when Nick's boys brought me in.

Adair says, "What's your name?"

"Sam," he says as if he has to think about it.

"Well, Sam," Adair says as if he's not really buying it, "if that's really your name, do you remember the other night when one of your guests went headfirst out the window?"

With another swallow, the clerk says, "Sure, I remember. The cops that were here already asked me all about it. I didn't know nothin', I didn't even know the guy."

"You have a hotel register? Any record of people signing in and signing out?"

Sam gives that a mean snicker. "In this dump? Look around. You really think our occupants matter enough to have names? They pay weekly, in cash, to a guy who comes around, and that's that."

I'm sure that's not quite that. That cash eventually makes its way into Sig's pocket.

Adair says, "Did you see anyone come in before it happened?"

"I mind my own business."

Adair and I both know we're not going to get anything useful from Sleepy Sam. We leave him to his slumbers, and walk upstairs to Nick's room.

Adair tries the door. It's locked.

"Gold?" he says without looking at me, not happy with his complicity in what he needs me to do.

I take my case of lockpicks from my jacket pocket and have us inside in mere seconds.

I turn on a lamp. The room hasn't changed since the night I was here, except for one thing: the window where Nick went out is boarded up, blocking the slashes of light from the flashing yellow ROOMS sign. That red chenille bedspread doesn't look nearly as menacing without the slashing light, though it's still nauseating.

Adair stands in the middle of the room, looks around. "I guess the Waldorf doesn't have to worry about any competition from this place." After that bit of wit, he gets to the business of studying the place. He's especially interested in the floor near the window, bends down close to have a look, rubs his fingers on the threadbare carpet. "No useful shoe prints, so I don't know if whoever gave Fortunato the shove was a big guy, little guy, or even a guy."

I say, "It would have to be a pretty strong woman to get the better of Nick and press him through the windowpane."

"You could do it," he says, looking up at me and smirking.

"But I didn't," I say.

"You know any more tough dames?" His smirk is even more annoying the second time.

"Sure, but they didn't do it, either."

He gives up on his joke and turns back to examining the carpet. "What's this?" He stands up, shows me a tiny clump, half the size of a dime, of curled yellow threads. "Sort of looks like hair, though of the cheap bottle variety," he says. "You see any bottle blondes when you were here? Maybe Fortunato ordered up a little, uhm, companionship for hire, if you know what I mean?"

"The only—" I stop talking and start thinking.

"What is it, Gold? You look like your horse is out front in the daily double at Belmont."

"You can ride with me or follow me in your car."

"And where are we going?"

"Just take that clump with you. But leave it in your pocket."

Chapter Twenty-Four

The small apartment building on East Twenty-eighth Street off Third Avenue isn't classy but isn't shabby, either. Just your average brick building for average New Yorkers making their dough doing average jobs, like insurance salesmen or schoolteachers, maybe an aspiring model or two. The occupant of apartment 503 is not the average tenant.

The door to apartment 503 opens after my repeated and heavy presses on the buzzer. In the light of the hallway, Chickie D'Andrea, his chubby face in need of a shave, his brown-and-white checked pajamas in need of ironing, is annoyed. "It's the middle of the goddamn night," he says, then nods toward Adair. "And who the hell are you?"

"It's only about half-past midnight, Chickie," I say. "You used to stay up 'til dawn tallying the odds and bets coming in from the hinterlands."

"Fine," Chickie says, "so for a few days I get to sleep like a regular citizen. So what. So what are you doing here, Cantor, and who the hell is this guy?"

I wait to make the introductions until Adair and I push our way past Chickie and I close and lock the door behind us. We're in the living room, where Chickie turns on a torch lamp that gives off a pale light that only barely reaches the corners of the room. The lamp's behind a side table next to a well-sat-in couch with somewhat lumpy cushions. The couch is salt-and-pepper gray, one of those nubby jobs good at hiding dropped cigarette and cigar ash. There's a couple of matching club chairs, also well sat in, a glass-topped coffee table with a heavy green glass ashtray that needs emptying, a red pack of Pall Malls and a book of matches beside it. Taking up most of a wall is what the furniture stores these days are calling a "home entertainment unit," meaning a long console—Chickie's is teakwood, probably veneer—with a TV, radio, and stereo record player built in. Except for a few cheap landscape prints in shiny metal frames, there's no art on the walls. All in all, not the ugliest room I've ever seen, just not a very refined one, sort of like its occupant.

"Chickie," I say, "meet Lieutenant Liam Adair of the New York City Police Department. Lieutenant Adair, meet Chickie D'Andrea, best oddsmaker in New York. The guy's got a head for numbers better than the agents at the IRS, who he scrupulously avoids."

Chickie's gone from merely annoyed at me to clearly wishing I was dead. "You bring a cop to my place? Is that how you play the game these days, Cantor? Are you—? Oh, sure, I get it. You're still steamed at me for giving you the brush-off on the phone." He plops down on the couch, the brown-and-white check of his pajamas battling with the nubby salt-and-pepper couch to decide which will give me a headache first. He takes a smoke from the pack of Pall Malls on the coffee table, lights it, exhales, and smiles at me through the smoke. "Well, you and your cop friend can just shove off."

"I'm disappointed in you, Chickie," I say. "What happened to the guy who wanted to help me find Nick's killer? What happened to the guy who owed Nick all kinds of gratitude for recognizing his talents and giving him a job?"

"Nothing happened to him," Chickie says. "He's just no

friend of yours anymore. Now beat it."

I'd laugh, but the guy's bluster is too pitiful to be funny. "Is this tough guy act one of your old vaudeville schticks, Chickie?" I say. "If it is, it's gone stale. It's time to come up with a new act; you know, where the nice guy honors his old pal Nick by cooperating with Nick's oldest friend and telling us what you know, or think you know, about who killed him. Even Lieutenant Adair might like that act, right, Lieutenant?"

Adair says, "Cut the crap," evidently not much of a show biz aficionado. "I think you'd know it's not a good idea to waste a cop's time, and you two are wasting my time but good. So listen, D'Andrea, if you know anything about who killed Fortunato, say so."

Bored by Adair's droning, I wander elsewhere in the living room, my attention caught by a framed photograph on a small table in a corner of the room, where the light of the torch lamp just barely reaches. Still, there's just enough light to see the photo of a smiling, alluring Abby O'Neill at some sort of social gathering. She appears to be listening to someone who's not in the photo. Maybe they never were, or maybe Chickie cut them out.

I walk back to Chickie and Adair, taking the photo with me. "Nice photo of Abby," I say. "You take the picture, Chickie?"

Chickie gets up from the couch, grabs the photo from my hands. "What if I did? It's none of your business, anyway," he says, and puts the photo on the side table.

Adair says, "If you want us out of your business, D'Andrea, just tell us what you know about Fortunato's killing, and we'll be out of here. If you don't come across, I can haul you in on a charge of withholding evidence."

Chickie gives that a spittle-edged little snigger. "You think I'd snitch?"

"You were going to tell Cantor, before you turned on her."

"Sure," Chickie says. "I figured I'd tell Cantor. We belong to the same club, y'know. We play by the same rules—or I thought we did," he says with a disgusted glance at me—"and those rules don't include cops. So haul me in, I don't care. My shyster will have me out in an hour."

Adair gives Chickie the kind of smile that scared you when you were a little kid, and still does. "But it will be an hour you'll never forget, D'Andrea."

The effect of Adair's smile on Chickie is something *I'll* never forget. I've never seen a guy's face—especially a plump face like Chickie's—seem to shrivel like a dried-out pear, and his body shrink to an airless blob inside his brown-and-white-checked pajamas.

It takes him a moment to get the air back into his lungs, giving him enough breath to get the miserable words out of his throat, "Okay, okay, just this one time I'll give over to a cop. But you gotta keep it to yourself. If it gets out that I snitched, I'm a dead man."

Adair says, "I know the game. Start talking."

Chickie looks at me, smiling a sneery smile. Then he looks at Adair, and finally back to me. "It was Mike. Mike Landers. He—"

I burst out laughing, a laugh so loud the neighbors might issue a noise complaint.

Chickie says, "What the hell's so funny, Gold?! You don't know Mike like I do. You don't know what kind of a guy he is."

I say, "I know he's a scared rabbit so worried about his own life he nearly drank himself into a permanent stupor the night Nick was killed."

"Sure he was scared," Chickie says with a theatrical wave of his hand. "He was scared of you. He was afraid you'd poke your nose where it didn't belong. There's things about Mike's life that aren't too kosher, y'know. No telling what he'd do to get you to stop pokin' around. And he has connections. Nasty connections, if you know what I mean, from his old days with the waterfront mob. I once heard him talk about a gunman up in—"

Adair jumps in, "Albany?"

"Yeah," Chickie says, grinning like a cooperative kid. "Yeah, Albany."

I give a quick look at Adair, and then it's my turn to jump in. "A guy named Stang? Or maybe Colnick?"

"Stang, yeah, I think."

Adair's face tells a story I'm glad he's not saying out loud. There's death in his eyes. Adair's the only cop I've ever known whose eyes don't usually carry a hint of death, at least they haven't until now. "I take it you know where Landers lives, Gold. Let's go."

"Hold on, Lieutenant," I say. I'm feeling a little sick to my stomach over the idea that Mike Landers, a guy I generally liked, a guy I felt sorry for, might've wanted me dead and maybe still does. But sick and angry as that makes me feel, it's a situation to deal with another time. I'm not finished here.

Chickie says, "Happy now, you two? Go get Mike Landers, toss his tush in jail, and let me get back to bed."

"Keep those eyes open a little while longer," I say.

Adair says, "We're wasting time with this nobody, Gold. Let's get Landers."

I say, "Lieutenant, take those yellow strands out of your pocket and give them to me."

He hands them over, impatient for me to get us out of here.

I show the yellow strands to Chickie, who reaches for them but I snatch them away.

He's annoyed. He's also gone pale. "How am I supposed to know what they are if you won't let me have a good look at them?" he says.

"You know what they are," I say. "And I think you know where Adair and I found them."

Chickie, nervous, bewildered, says, "You got into the trunk of my car? That's where I keep my costume stuff."

Now it's Adair who looks bewildered, if only for a moment, as his cop brain starts to put things together. Almost. He flashes me an inquisitive look.

I say, "Did you know, Lieutenant, that Mr. Chickie D'Andrea was once one of vaudeville's finest performers? Specialized in silly impersonations and crazy costumes. Still keeps his hand in the show biz trade with low-rent lodge meetings and birthday parties and the like. Only the birthday party he gave Nick didn't have a lotta laughs. Oh sure, Chickie showed up in a costume and a wig, only Nick didn't recognize him. Neither did I. Why would I recognize that the poor old Apple Annie in the shabby clothes and tangled blond hair I saw getting off the elevator was that washed-up entertainer Chickie D'Andrea? How did you find Nick, Chickie?"

"You're nuts, Cantor. Maybe you should be in show business, write the jokes."

I say again, colder this time, and grab the photo of Abby. "How did you find Nick, Chickie?"

He stands up from the couch, reaches for the photo, but I snap it away.

I say again, "How did you find Nick, Chickie? I already know why you killed him. I just want to know how smart you were to find him."

He grabs for the photo again, but again I pull it away fast. Turning just as fast, he opens the drawer in the side table and pulls out a .38 revolver, points it back and forth at me and Adair. He looks idiotic: a gunman in wrinkled pajamas, and with tears in his eyes and spittle at the corners of his mouth. "I heard Nick's guys talk about getting instructions from Nick to grab you," he says, trying hard not to cry like a baby, "so I followed them, saw them hustle you into their car and drive you away. When they got you to that crummy hotel in the Bronx and walked in, I put on my outfit and waited in my car until I was sure no one else was coming."

I say, "She didn't tell you to do it, Chickie. She didn't tell you to kill Nick."

Adair says, "Who didn't tell him? What are you talking about, Gold?"

"The woman in this picture," I say, handing him the framed photo. "Abby O'Neill. The woman who's taking over Nick's operation—and then some. Chickie's blind-as-a-bat in love with her. I guess he figured he'd score lovey-dovey points with her to get rid of Nick so that she could move in."

Adair says, "But she didn't mind you poking around?"

"I guess she figured she could handle me," I say. Well, maybe she could, I say to myself with a silent laugh. All I say out loud is, "It's over, Chickie. Put the gun down."

"The hell I will," he says, his voice quiet but edging up to shrill. "I'm not looking to fry in the chair up in Sing Sing, and I don't wanna spend the rest of my life in some cell there, either. I want a deal. There's stuff I know. Listen, Lieutenant, the stuff I could tell you, you'll arrest half of New York, and maybe even get your captain's stripes. So whaddya say?"

It's me, not Adair who answers. "You know there are people who won't let that happen, Chickie." I don't mention Sig's name. I don't have to. "Give me the gun, Chickie," I say, and take a step closer.

"No. You and this cop are dead. I know places to bury you where you'll never be found."

Adair and I look at each other, swamp memories between us.

Adair also gives me a flick with his eyes toward Chickie.

I get the message.

I take another step toward Chickie.

He looks straight at me, says, "Don't, Cantor. I'll shoot you dead, I will."

"And you think Abby will like that? She didn't want Nick killed and she doesn't want me dead, either."

"Why?" he sneers, his eyes bulging and staring at me. "You

think you can make time with her? Hah! She's not a pervert like you, Cantor. But it won't matter, anyway. No one will miss you."

He's so focused on me, he doesn't see Adair's hand slide into his coat, or the gun that comes out and Adair raises high, then slams down on the back of Chickie's head.

Adair doesn't stop me when I get out of there fast while he calls into his precinct, reports the incident, and requests an ambulance. I'm downstairs and in my Buick before he even hangs up.

After all the recent death, all the secrets, and the crushing news that it was Mike Landers who nearly sent me into the swamp—he'll be in Adair's clutches soon enough—I need life, I need Lily.

It's nearly one-thirty in the morning when I park in front of her hotel. When I'm in the lobby, heading for the elevators, the night clerk at the desk, a classier guy than the Cortland Hotel's Sleepy Sam, calls out, "Just a moment! Are you a guest here? Where do you think you're going at this hour?"

"Miss Vardanian's room. I know my way."

"You're too late."

"Maybe she's still awake. I'll knock quietly. I won't disturb your other guests on the hall."

"No, I mean she's not there. She checked out this afternoon."

The bullet Chickie almost put in my chest would hurt less than what the desk clerk just said.

There's no one to blame but myself. If I'd let Lily keep her secrets last night, I might've been able to keep her in my bed, and my life.

Lily Vardanian's no fool. I'm the fool.

Chapter Twenty-Five

After a lousy night's sleep, it seems I've wrestled my sheets in a do-or-die match I barely won. Or maybe I didn't. Maybe I'm dead, which might explain why the sharp, hot needles of water in my shower are having a tough time kicking me into gear.

My muscles and bones eventually take charge, though, insisting they're alive, which means that I am, too.

When I step out of the shower and into the living room, there's a raucous rock-'n'-roll song playing on the radio, some wild man banging on a piano and shouting about a whole lotta shakin'. I've heard the song before, usually get a kick out of it, but not this morning, not after that rotten night's sleep that's left me at the edge of a headache. I'm about to turn the dial to find a tune more soothing when an announcer cuts in: *"We interrupt this program to bring you a special report."* The next voice I hear is a familiar one, familiar to me and to millions of New Yorkers who tune into the eleven o'clock TV news each night. *"Hello,"* he says, *"this is John C. Vanderhyde. Most of you are more accustomed to seeing and hearing me just before your bedtime, not early in the morning. But tonight will be different. You will not see me or hear me on your local television dial. I am here this morning to tell you that I have just been fired for daring to cross the bigwigs*

I don't need to hear any more.

Lily.

I have no doubt that Sig has the documents. They'll never see the light of day, which will make the police department very happy, not to mention various shady members of the City Council. Sig might even burn the documents, though on second thought I doubt it. They could be useful to him someday. There's power in having the goods on people. Dirty laundry as coin.

How Lily got the documents is anyone's guess. I don't want to think about her possibly playing footsie or some other bodily pattycake with Vanderhyde. I soothe my jealous heart, if only a little, remembering that Vanderhyde's rumored to be the goody-goody type, an arrow so straight he's resistant even to life's juicier temptations. But however Lily pinched the papers, her smooth fingers are what she gets paid the big bucks for, and what protects her.

She doesn't need me.

Acknowledgements

Writing a book is a solitary activity. You're alone—well, except for the characters and their voices in your head. But it takes a crowd to see the endeavor through: friends who assure you you're brilliant; editors who also assure you you're brilliant even when they find holes in your plot and spelling errors one usually leaves behind in the third grade; and publishers who hold the fate of your aforementioned brilliance in their hands. Without any of these folks, all of whom have propped me up through the struggle known as being a writer, this book would not have made the leap from my computer screen to the print copy in your hands or the ebook you take on vacation.

So, here's the crowd to whom I owe my genuinely heartfelt thanks: cherished friends Jody Gray, Jackie Hawley, Stan Coplan, Jan Schleiger, Renée Bess, Barry Katz, Mitchell Karp, Cora Jane Glasser, Anne Finkelstein, Fran Beallor, Dan Gluck, Jacqueline Burke, Kate Fitzgerald, Claudine Dumoulin, Claude Pollack, Sabine Pollack Merle for the morning laughs from across the sea, with special thanks to Nalda Rodriguez for reconnecting with my life and my heart. Thanks to my editor Paula Martinac for her sensitive reading, and copyeditor Elizabeth Andersen for her respect for an author's voice. Deepest thanks to the gang at Bywater Books—ever-patient publisher Salem West, brilliant cover designer Ann McMan, and dearest Marianne K. Martin— for their faith in me. And as always, my fine pal and hometown New York anchor Allan Neuwirth, my "Noo Yawk Bagel Bro."

About the Author

Native New Yorker Ann Aptaker's Cantor Gold crime/mystery series has won Lambda Literary and Goldie Awards. Her short stories have appeared in two editions of the *Fedora* crime anthology, *Crime Ink: Iconic, Switchblade Magazine's Stiletto Heeled* issue, the *Mickey Finn: Twenty-First Century Noir* anthology Volume 1 and Volume 3, and in *Black Cat Mystery Magazine*. Her short story, "Neon Women," was selected for inclusion in the 2025 Best American Mystery and Suspense anthology. Her novella, *A Taco, A T-Bird, A Barretta and One Furious Night,* was published by Down & Out Books for their *Guns And Tacos* crime series. Her flash fiction, *A Night In Town*, appeared in the online zine *Punk Soul Poet,* and another flash fiction, *Rock 'N Dyke Roll,* is featured in the Goldie Award winning anthology *Happy Hours: Our Lives in Gay Bars.* Ann has been an art curator, exhibition design specialist, art writer, and was a professor of Art History at the New York Institute of Technology. She now writes full time.

The 2024 Foreword INDIES Publisher of the Year award was presented to Bywater Books for its twenty years of ushering in the "coming of age of queer literature."

"In a year when LGBTQ+ communities faced renewed attacks and the names of DEI efforts were sullied by those in power, Bywater remained firm in its commitment to publishing titles that celebrate queer existence and that embrace diversity. Their world-widening books make us laugh, make us cry, and stand as enduring testaments to the breadth of love and the human experience."

– Foreword Reviews

Bywater Books believes that all people have the right to read or not read what they want—and that we are all entitled to make those choices ourselves. But to ensure these freedoms, books and information must remain accessible. Any effort to eliminate or restrict these rights stands in opposition to freedom of choice.

Please join us by opposing book bans and censorship of the LGBTQ+ and BIPOC communities.

At Bywater Books, we are all stories.

For more information about Bywater Books, our publishing mission, authors, and our titles, please visit our website.

https://bywaterbooks.com